"I'm not bad for a snooty dame from a magazine?" Abby asked archly.

"Snootiness never looked so good," Mick agreed. His grin was easy. "A minute ago, you looked like you were going to faint, though," he teased.

"I never interviewed a naked man before. If you had reached for your zipper, I was ready to run!" Did the man have the right to look so darned sexy?

"Are you fainthearted beneath that Greta Garbo exterior?" he shot back.

"Greta Garbo?"

"Sure. I fell for her when I was twelve. She was always very sophisticated. You're a lot like her."

Abby lifted her nose. "I vant to be alone."

He laughed. "Very provocative—even for grown-up boys." He reached for his shirt . . .

Other Second Chance at Love books by
Elissa Curry

Elissa Curry is a former teacher of gifted students who now employs her own gifts for writing sparkling dialogue and creating inventive plots as a romance author. She lives with her husband and their two young daughters in Indiana, Pennsylvania. The secret of Elissa's compelling romances? "I turn on the music and my word processor, and the stories seem to write themselves."

Dear Reader:

Summer may be ending, but this month's SECOND CHANCE AT LOVE romances will keep the fun alive. We begin with...

Anything Goes (#286) by Diana Morgan. This is the fifteenth romance—but a first for SECOND CHANCE AT LOVE—by this husband-and-wife writing team. And what a zany romp it is! Angie Carpenter, who's just been named Supermom by a national magazine, becomes so incensed by wily inventor Kyle Bennett that she vows to uphold housewives and the American way by beating Kyle's six-armed robot in a televised contest. But she doesn't reckon on falling in love with Kyle! *Anything Goes* boasts what must be one of the most original reasons for interrupting a love scene—Benny the robot arrives unexpectedly to serve lunch! Angie's mortified. You, on the other hand, may never stop laughing.

Poisoned peanut butter may sound like a "sticky" basis for a romance, but in *Sophisticated Lady* (#287) Elissa Curry adds a mouth-watering hero and a never-stuck-up heroine to create a delicious love story. The problem is that Mick Piper's being accused of poisoning his *own* peanut butter (he manufactures the stuff), and Abigail Vanderbine, who's come to interview him and ends up staying, is determined to find out who's really responsible. You'll find Elissa's magic touch in the gleefully witty repartee and oh, so sexy situations. And be sure not to miss the cameo appearance by Grace and Luke Lazurnovich from Elissa's *Lady Be Good* (#247)!

In *The Phoenix Heart* (#288) by Betsy Osborne, proper Bostonian Alyssa Courtney is sure she'll never adjust to laid-back, freaked-out California—especially once she meets gulpingly handsome cartoonist Rade Stone. Suddenly she's living in a state of constant crisis, and falling in love with a man whom her job requires she expose as an evil influence on children! Even her kids turn traitors by being on their worst behavior around Rade. Don't miss this tenderly warm romance filled with laughter and loving.

In *Fallen Angel* (#289), Carole Buck creates a powerfully emotional love story. Beautiful, vulnerable Mallory Victor is caught between two worlds: the upper-crust New England world of hero Dr. David Hitchcock, and the glittery but ultimately shallow world of rock music—where, unknown to David, she induces hysteria in teen-aged fans as rock's "bad girl," Molly V. Using both Mallory's and David's points of view to very skillful effect, Carole deeply involves us in these two characters' dilemma. Carole says *she* cried as she wrote the last thirty pages. Maybe you'd better keep some tissues handy, just in case...

Hilary Cole adds a fresh voice to romances in *The Sweetheart Trust* (#290). Here, the desirous thoughts of two mystery writers put zing into their literary collaboration. Kate Fairchild has already fallen hard for impossibly charming, delightfully unpredictable, infuriatingly witty Nick Trent. When she inherits a decrepit Victorian mansion, she seizes the opportunity to domesticate Nick in a country setting. But rural life includes unexpected—often hilarious—complications ... and none of the guarantees Kate's looking for. Lots of you raved about Hilary Cole's TO HAVE AND TO HOLD romance, *My Darling Detective* (#34). You'll be even more enchanted by *The Sweetheart Trust*.

Finally, in *Dear Heart* (#291) we bring you a delightful new tale from an old favorite, Lee Williams. Why does Charly Lynn gravitate toward children and lovingly nurture the animals in the pet store she helps run? Bret Roberts doesn't have time to find out. He's too busy stealing kisses ... and trying to survive the antics of a hysterical monkey in little red pants who decides to take someone's car for a joy ride on a San Francisco hill! The fact that Bret is allergic to animals—and Charly houses innumerable dogs, cats, a rabbit, and a parakeet in her small apartment—complicates the rocky romance between this hapless couple, who are otherwise perfect for each other. Or almost ... When things get really rough, Charly writes to "Dear Mr. Heart," the local advice columnist, begging for help ... never realizing what further trouble she's getting into!

Enjoy! Warm wishes,

Ellen Edwards

Ellen Edwards, Senior Editor
SECOND CHANCE AT LOVE
The Berkley Publishing Group
200 Madison Avenue
New York, NY 10016

Second Chance at Love

SOPHISTICATED LADY

ELISSA CURRY

**SECOND CHANCE AT LOVE
BOOK**

First edition published September 1985

First printing

"Second Chance at Love" and the butterfly emblem are trademarks
belonging to Jove Publications, Inc.

Printed in the United States of America

Second Chance at Love books are published by
The Berkley Publishing Group
200 Madison Avenue, New York, NY 10016

With thanks to
DR. DEBRA PIKE

SOPHISTICATED LADY

CHAPTER ONE

"PEANUT BUTTER!" Abby exclaimed, astonished.

"I'm not telling you to do something disgusting with it," growled her father as he glared at her over the silver rims of his glasses. "I'm asking you to find out about the man who makes it."

"But—heavens, *peanut* butter!"

"Put aside your preconceived snobbery and take a broader view of things. Maybe these country folk can teach you something."

A story about peanut butter wasn't the kind of thing *The Epicurean* magazine usually published, which was why Abigail Vanderbine was more than a little puzzled to find herself assigned to report on the product manufactured by a small West Virginia–based company known as Piper's Peanut Butter.

Abby had hoped for something a little more exciting for her first assignment, but being the boss's daughter had disadvantages. In his declining years, Abby's father was not only developing increasingly pedestrian tastes, but his tyrannical attitudes toward employees and family alike were getting even worse.

"An interview like this will get you into the swing of how *we* do things," he told her, no doubt obliquely referring to her short-lived career in newspaper writing and a recently blown love affair involving a fellow reporter. "And a character like this Piper fellow might teach you a little something about how the other half lives, too!"

What was *that* supposed to mean? Abby wondered. Since when was Harry Vanderbine, curmudgeon *extraordinaire,* interested in anyone who wasn't frequently named in the society pages? But Abby wisely held her tongue and dutifully flew to Charleston, West Virginia, to start her research.

Arriving in the village of Blue Creek, she easily found the offices of Piper's Peanut Butter, since the town consisted of little more than half a dozen houses, a gas station, a supermarket, and the brick-faced factory buildings of Piper's. Abby parked her rental car under the blossoming apple trees, checked her makeup, smoothed her linen suit, collected her camera equipment and materials, and then climbed a set of wooden steps that had been painted precisely the same vivid yellow as the lid on a jar of the Piper product. She opened the glass-paned door and heard the resulting cheery jingle of a bell. Although the bell had undoubtedly been hung there to announce arrivals, there was no one in the modest reception room to greet Abby that morning.

She entered hesitantly and was oddly reluctant to close the door behind herself. She cleared her throat delicately and called, "Hello? Is anyone here?"

The place appeared to be deserted. A desk in the middle of the small room was cluttered with papers and looked as if it hadn't been occupied in weeks. A row of peanut-butter jars decorated the top of a battered filing cabinet, and Abby was willing to wager that those jars hadn't been dusted since the days of Eisenhower. A plate abandoned on the windowsill, complete with the half-eaten remains of a peanut-butter sandwich, was the only sign of recent habitation.

Ever hopeful, Abby closed the door and called louder this time, "Hello! Anyone home?"

A thump resounded from not too far away, and suddenly the office door adjoining the reception area was jerked open from within. A man stuck his head out. A big man. A very big man in jeans and a plaid shirt.

"Hi," he said, almost breathless. He jerked his head. "I've got ten minutes, that's it. Come in."

And he disappeared again.

Abby took a deep breath and prayed she could live up to the Vanderbine standards of journalistic excellence in the face of adversity. It was now or never. Head high, she stepped smartly across the planked floor and through the door that was painted with the name of the occupant: MICHAEL J. PIPER, PRESIDENT. Inside, a radio played rock and roll.

He was busy in his office, rummaging through an open drawer of another filing cabinet, this one topped by a yellow hard hat instead of jars of peanut butter. He was roughly dressed and impatient. "Come on, come on," he urged, not bothering to look over his shoulder at her. "Let's get started, huh? I'm runnin' late today."

"Very well, Mr. Piper," Abby said composedly, hoping she sounded as genteel as the rest of the Vanderbine women. "I believe we spoke on the telephone Thursday. My name is—"

"Yeah, yeah," he interrupted over the music. "I remember. Listen, you're going to have to bear with us around here for a while. My secretary just had a baby, and we're tryin' to run things without her until she gets back, and it's— Damn, where could she have put that— Ah! Terrific!" He slammed the file drawer and turned toward Abby. He was visibly startled by her appearance and promptly stared at her, eyes wide.

Abby returned the stare, equally taken aback by what confronted her. She had expected a middle-aged executive in a three-piece suit. Michael J. Piper was only in his thirties, and he dressed like a much younger man— jeans, a flannel shirt with the sleeves rolled up around his elbows, a pair of white leather basketball shoes haphazardly laced. His hair was dark and cut short—not stylishly, but in a way that made Abby suspect that he submitted to a barber infrequently and between visits allowed his straight hair to grow into a thick mop. His face was tan and clean-shaven, marked by dark straight brows, deepset eyes that were deceptively half-lidded, and a once-aristocratic nose undoubtedly broken—perhaps even during a fist fight. He looked as though he could be a tough customer if he wanted to be. He had a slightly crooked mouth with a full lower lip that curved wickedly when he grinned. The unlit stub of a cigar was clamped between his teeth.

He grinned around the cigar when he'd finished sizing her up. She had worn a brand-new linen suit the color of iced lemonade with an expensively simple white cotton blouse underneath and a string of pearls as suggested by her mother. Her hair was ash blond, and she had painstakingly swept it back and upward into a neat French-braided twist. Abby knew that she looked cool and pristine, for she had checked her makeup in the car to make absolutely sure her appearance was utterly apropos for this occasion. Her lipstick was applied flawlessly for once, outlining the perfect bow that was the hereditary Vanderbine mouth. After all, she was representing *The Epicurean* now and had to look the part. At twenty-six, Abby had finally contrived to look like the rest of the Vanderbines—cool, sedate, intellectual, and—above all—classy.

The expression on Michael J. Piper's face was not exactly complimentary, however. He looked amused by the startling contrast her beautifully groomed appearance made to his cluttered office. "Forgive me," he said, almost drawling. He took out his cigar and tried without success to smother his smile. "You're spiffier than I expected, that's all. Have you been to the factory yet?"

Abby's pride was stung by his frank amusement at her appearance, but she summoned her poise. Be serene and professional during an interview, Mother had coached, emphasizing that writing for a gourmet magazine was different from a beat on a newspaper. Pasting what she hoped was a poised smile on her face, Abby said, "No, I haven't, Mr. Piper. I thought it would be best to start with you."

"Oh, sure." He nodded and gestured at his desk with the file folder he held. "Put your gear there, if you like. What do you want to know? My whole history, I suppose?"

"Yes, exactly," Abby replied, and she moved to put her camera and equipment case on the edge of his desk. "Afterward, perhaps I could go to the factory."

"Sure thing. We're all set to cooperate, y'know."

"That's very kind." Abby began to unfasten the latches on her equipment case and said, "Perhaps I ought to hear a little about you first?"

He strolled behind his desk, but didn't sit down. He was soaking in a first impression and taking his time doing so. Dropping the file folder, he cocked his head ingenuously and asked, "The whole thing right now, huh? You don't want to give me any time to get nervous, is that it?"

Abby smiled again, pulling the microphone cord out of the case. She was going to have to be careful not to succumb to this character's country-boy charm. Coolly, she assured him, "There's no need to be nervous. I'm painless, you'll see. Shall we begin?"

He shrugged and dropped his cigar into the nearest ashtray. "You're the doctor," he said flippantly. "What do you want to know? I'm thirty-four, with a clean bill of health so far. I've owned the company for five years, so I'm mostly at my desk now. I used to work in the factory when I was a teenager—that was when it belonged to my uncle—and then I spent some time working as the foreman when I got out of college—still manual stuff. Now I'm much more—what's the matter?"

He had been unbuttoning his shirt! During his monologue, he had calmly unfastened the buttons down the front of his faded shirt. Abby's face must have given away her frank amazement. He slowly tugged his shirttail out of his jeans, ready to strip off the garment entirely. Then he stopped altogether, noticing her expression.

Abby hastily busied herself with her tape recorder. What kind of place had she stumbled into? Father had certainly meant what he said when he ordered her to start at the bottom of the magazine ladder. This peanut-butter king was not the usual *Epicurean* fodder. Still, Abby was determined to get a good interview. Michael J. Piper could stand on his head and wiggle his toes for all she cared—just so he gave her some good stuff for her article.

"N-nothing's the matter, Mr. Piper." She tried to smile up at him and said, "Please go ahead. I'll be ready with this equipment any minute."

"Okay." He stripped off his shirt in one effortless, casual motion, with the air of a man who was perfectly comfortable undressing in front of a strange woman. Dropping the garment over the back of his chair, he said curiously, "You know, I get the feeling you don't do this kind of thing very often."

"Well, I admit this is a change of scenery for me," Abby replied honestly, keeping her head down to hide her dismay. He was naked to the waist! Trying not to be flustered by the unexpected, she said, "But I assure you that I know exactly what I'm doing."

He sauntered back around the desk toward her. "What do you think of us so far?"

Abby instinctively shrunk down into her chair. "The company? Well, I haven't done much research yet, of course." He hadn't intended his question to be a double entendre, surely? As she stared at his chest, Abby's hands fumbled the tape recorder, struggling to plug in the mike. She was actually nervous!

He came close and sat down on the edge of the desk beside her equipment case. His shoulders were golden in the spring sunlight that streamed in from the tall windows behind his desk. On his chest, he had a T-shaped scattering of almost blond hair that looked like it might be crisp to the touch. And there was a subtle scent of masculine skin in the air suddenly, just enough that Abby's sensitive nose could detect it through the acrid smell of cigars. He wasn't the kind of man to wear after-shave lotions. Nor was he the kind of man who was coy with his body, for he looked perfectly at ease without his shirt. A little thick around the waist, but not paunchy.

Michael J. Piper wasn't oblivious to Abby's unconscious reaction to him. He sat still and waited expectantly, with an unmistakable gleam in his eyes. He actually seemed to be enjoying her dismay for a few seconds. Then he relented and said kindly, "Listen, this is no big deal, is it? I think you're more nervous than I am!"

"I'm not nervous," Abby insisted at once, determined to keep her cool in the face of anything. "I just— Look, Mr. Piper, would you mind—"

"Do you want some help? I hate to see you blush like that when—"

"I am not blushing!" she snapped in spite of herself.

"Okay, okay, I just thought it might be easier on you if I did the—well, whatever you do with the electrodes."

His eyes, she realized suddenly as she stared into them, were perfectly gray. Blankly, she repeated, "Electrodes?"

"Whatever they're called. I've been having some very kinky nightmares about them ever since we talked earlier, and now that I've seen you, I— Look, I haven't got much time. You see, there's some dame from a snooty magazine coming later, so if you want me to help with this exam, I'd be—" He stopped himself, suddenly matching her blank expression with one of his own. He realized he had made a mistake.

Carefully, Abby said, "Mr. Piper, I think there's been a misunderstanding."

He let out a long breath, looking as if he'd just been caught in the wrong locker room by the school principal. "You're not the girl from the medical school, are you?"

"No," Abby said politely, hiding a smile. She couldn't resist. "I'm the dame from the snooty magazine."

CHAPTER TWO

FORTUNATELY, MICHAEL J. PIPER began to laugh. He stayed on the edge of the desk and roared, shaking his head. "I'm sorry, really I am. You must think I'm— Judas, what an idiot! I thought you were from the university. They're doing research about the effects of peanut butter on the cardiovascular system, and we volunteered to be their guinea pigs for the study. I thought this was the portable electrocardiogram thing she was telling me about!"

"It's my tape recorder and camera, that's all. I'm sorry, this is my fault. I should have introduced myself properly. I'm Abigail Vanderbine, from *The Epicurean* magazine."

"Of course," he said with a beguiling sweetness that seemed natural even for a man as big as he was. He put out his hand. "How do you do, Miss Vanderbine? I'm Mick Piper."

Abby stood up and accepted his handshake, and her

fingers were at once enclosed by his firm, very warm hand. "I'm glad to meet you, Mr. Piper," she said with a genuine smile. "We spoke briefly on the telephone last week."

"I remember now," he replied, a crooked grin on his mouth. His eyes were lively beneath those lazy lashes, watching her face for an instant before sliding swiftly down her body to appraise once more. He didn't try to hide what he was doing, but gave her a thorough inspection, saying, "You sounded a lot different on the phone, I must say. I didn't picture you looking like this."

"I'm afraid to ask how you did picture me," Abby said spontaneously, "if thinking about electrodes was enough to give you kinky nightmares."

He grinned. "I pictured you older. Stuffier," he added, unabashedly truthful as he held her gaze with his. "And not nearly so attractive. You sounded awfully formal on the phone. Looking like this, though . . . you might provide even kinkier dreams than electrodes, Miss Vanderbine."

"I'm not bad for a snooty dame from a magazine, is that it?" she asked archly.

"Snootiness never looked so good," Mick agreed, still clasping her hand in his. His grin was easy, his eyes dancing with light. He liked her ability to bounce back, it seemed. "A minute ago, you looked like you were going to faint, though," he teased.

"I never interviewed a naked man before. If you had reached for your zipper, I was ready to run!"

He laughed again and let go of her hand, getting lithely to his feet. He turned down the volume on the radio and said, "I've never been interviewed at all before, you know, except by the local paper four years ago when we had a strike at the factory. I nearly had to strip down for that one, but only figuratively. Should I get dressed again, or—"

"I'm the fainthearted type," Abby warned before he could suggest an alternative. Did the man have the right to look so—well, so darned sexy for her first assignment on her father's elegant magazine?

"Are you really fainthearted beneath that Greta Garbo exterior?" he shot back.

"Greta Garbo?"

"Sure. I fell for her when I was twelve. She was always very sophisticated. You're a lot like her."

Abby managed to control her smile and lifted her nose. "I vant to be alone."

"That's it!" He laughed. "Very provocative—even for grown-up boys." He reached for his shirt. "Just to be on the safe side, though, how about if you and I start all over again?"

"Yes, please," she said with a smile, abandoning her Garbo impression and hoping she was keeping her skittering heart a secret. Why did she feel so exhilarated? It was as if adrenaline were shooting through her veins. "I'm in way over my head!" she admitted.

He laughed at her expression and said, "Okay, tell me why you're here."

Abby switched on her tape recorder and sat down in the nearest chair, hoping that she had collected her poise completely. Agreeably, she explained, "Our magazine is doing a series of stories about foods that are uniquely American. Last month we covered the subject of clam chowder pretty thoroughly, and one of my colleagues is working on a piece about fried chicken. Our editor suggested I check out peanut butter, and we understand that your product is considered the epitome of old-fashioned American peanut butter. Besides, you're a small, family-owned company, and that's the kind of angle that's interesting to our readers."

He nodded, taking his time getting into his shirt again. "They'd rather not hear about a conglomerate that's making both food and petroleum under the same roof?"

"Exactly." Abby smothered her grin and hoped she could go on behaving herself. Remembering her mother's exhortations, she sat up straight and said, *"The Epicurean* is a specialty magazine, Mr. Piper. We like to elevate food to—well, almost to an art form."

"Peanut butter?" he asked, looking skeptical and bemused. "You want to make peanut butter into art?"

"Well," Abby corrected solicitously, "we'd like to try."

Watching Michael J. Piper button up his shirt and tuck it back into his jeans again, she began to think that the man was a little like the product he manufactured. He had no frills. He wasn't fancy. He was honest and probably wholesome and a little sweet, and yet he was—well, nutritious. He looked like an all-American boy who had made it big by his own hard work. And the name Mick suited him. He didn't refer to himself as Michael J., which a different kind of executive might do. He called himself Mick and had no pretenses.

He considered sitting down on the plain swivel chair behind the desk, but he glanced at Abby and obviously changed his mind. He came back around the desk to where she sat. Standing over her, he asked abruptly, "What's your name again?"

"Abigail Vanderbine."

He pretended to wince. "That sounds like the good-manners lady. Dear Abby Vanderbilt."

"No, the etiquette writer is Amy Vanderbilt, and Dear Abby is Abigail Van Buren, the advice columnist."

"I stand corrected," he said with a grin. He picked up the hard hat that was perched on the top of the filing cabinet. "Okay, Dear Abby, when was the last time you ate peanut butter?"

"Oh, years ago, I'm afraid."

He nodded, spinning the hat on his hand. "I believe it. You look like the caviar type, all right. You don't keep a jar of Piper's in your house, do you?"

"No, I'm afraid not."

"You have any kids?"

Startled by that, Abby said, "No, I'm not married."

He grinned again and winked. "When you get around to having kids, I bet even you will start keeping peanut butter in the house. It's the original convenience food."

"Do *you* like peanut butter?" Abby asked, trying to take charge of the interview before he wrested complete control from her.

"Love it," he declared. "On bread, on crackers, on fruit, on anything. I'm an addict and have been since before I was three years old. Come on. It's time for me to go have a look around the floor, and you may as well come along. Here, put this on. Safety regulations apply to visitors, too."

The hard hat was bright yellow, the official Piper Peanut Butter color, it seemed. Abby accepted the hat hesitantly. She hadn't been prepared to let down her hair during the interview, and she was a little nervous about giving up her newly acquired professional manners even for a moment. She was aware that Mick Piper was watching indulgently. To get a good story, she might as well play along. She put on the hat.

"Terrible fit," he noted bluntly with a grin, "but it looks good on you, I think. Do you suppose you could get away with a hat like that at your next charity ball?"

Abby smiled wryly at him, and she got to her feet.
"Only if it had a feather. You're enjoying this, aren't
you?"

"Seeing a sophisticated lady like yourself in a peanut-
butter factory for the first time? You bet. It makes me
think you might be convinced to try a few other things.
This way, Dear Abby. Let's see what you think of the
place."

Abby had to hurry after Mick Piper; she realized that
she had better move fast or risk getting left behind. Though
he had mistakenly pegged her for a much poised woman,
he made no concessions to female frailties. As they went
out through the front door and down the steps, Mick
clattered ahead of her and led the way across a short
stretch of gravel driveway. Abby was slower in the nar-
row-heeled pumps she was unaccustomed to wearing.

"We could have gone downstairs and over to the factory underground, but it's such a nice day that I like to
get outside now and then," Mick explained. "The plant
is pretty noisy. Think you can stand it for a few minutes?"

"Do I have a choice?"

"We've got earplugs," he suggested, smiling again.
"But they'd clash with your outfit."

Wry again, Abby sent him a mock glare. "Lead the
way, Mr. Piper. I'll shout when I'm ready to surrender."

"Oooh, good," he said on an unaffected laugh. "She's
talking about surrendering to me already! This way."

He shouldered open a double swinging door and led
Abby into the ear-splitting din of the peanut-butter factory. A portly, ruddy-faced man with a big grin greeted
them near the door, and Mick made shouted introduc-
tions. Abby thought the red-faced man was called Frank,
but she wasn't sure. He was the foreman, she guessed.

Mick sent him for a second hard hat, which was quickly produced from a cupboard.

The peanut-butter factory was a complicated tangle of huge stainless-steel tanks and pipes, conveyor belts, and gigantic, noisy machines. There was a bizarre apparatus that shook violently, which, Mick shouted into her ear, was called a gravity separator. A peanut roaster came next, a very long, tall metal box that gave off a mouth-watering fragrance of newly roasted nuts. Next came a blancher, which rubbed off the skins of the peanuts. After being sorted, Mick explained in a bellow, the nuts were ground, mixed with other ingredients, and finally squished through a big tube to the bottling assembly line.

"The labels are put on the jars in the packing room," he explained in her ear. "We sell peanut butter to grocery chains who want us to put their labels on the jars. Only about half of what we make actually goes out with our own name on it."

Abby stood in the thunderous room and watched the empty glass jars come trundling down a conveyor belt like little soldiers. They were filled with just the right amount of peanut butter before whirling through a machine that planted a bright-yellow lid on the top of each jar. The sight made Abby ridiculously pleased, for some reason. She stood there smiling, mesmerized by the sight of those warm jars, each headed for a different American household where it would be emptied by cherubic little children.

When he had finished a shouted conversation with one of his employees, Mick Piper plucked a jar of peanut butter from the assembly line and took Abby's arm with his other hand. He guided her out through a set of doors and into a foyer where a basket of bread loaves had been set near the door. Mick grabbed one and shouldered the next door wide. Then they were suddenly outside in the sunshine again.

Abby's ears were ringing. She shook her head hard and smiled up at Mick. "That was wonderful!"

"You liked it?" he asked, delighted. "It always makes people smile the way you're doing now—all misty-eyed and sentimental."

Abby looked away, but said cheerfully, "You ought to give tours."

He shrugged and led her across the grass. "We bring the local kindergarten kids through here every year, and some students from the university are always coming around trying to show us how to improve our efficiency. Hungry?"

After inhaling the fragrance of roasting peanuts, Abby felt suddenly famished. She nodded. "Yes, as a matter of fact, I am."

He still had a grasp on her elbow, a touch that was natural and perhaps possessive. He guided her to a picnic table that stood conveniently under a blossom-laden apple tree. "Prepare yourself for a gourmet's treat, Dear Abby. There's nothing that compares with peanut butter fresh off the line. Except maybe basketball and a few things you have to take your clothes off for, but I . . . Damn, but you blush easily, don't you?"

"It's the sunshine, that's all."

"Of course. How foolish of me not to realize." He laughed and then commanded, "Sit down, now. Watch for splinters. Open that jar, will you? I usually carry a sterilized knife for such situations, but today you're just going to have to close your eyes and pretend you don't see this." He pulled a Swiss army knife from out of his hip pocket and flicked open the longest blade. He swiped it across the thigh of his jeans a few times and then used it to slice off a chunk of bread. Abby knew that the sterilized-knife story was a fib, for Mick's technique with the pocket knife was practiced. "Whole wheat today," he announced when he broke through the crust.

"Fresh bread to go with the peanut butter?"

"Sure. We're strictly first class around here. The bakery up the road delivers a dozen loaves every morning. My sister runs the bakery. Her son drives the truck."

"Convenient."

"Also free. Here." He used the same knife to slather the piece of bread with peanut butter, looking like an exuberant, overgrown Huck Finn for a brief moment. Then, with a sweeping bow that turned him into a man again, he passed the treat into Abby's waiting hands. He stood back to watch. "Well?"

Abby took a delicate bite. Crisp bread and the sweet warmth of peanuts melted on her tongue. She closed her eyes instinctively and savored the taste that sent her plummeting back into her childhood. She remembered a toasty kitchen on a winter's morning, with the cook making muffins and Mother and Father sipping coffee behind their newspapers, reading the comics aloud. The peanut butter made her tongue thick, so her response was garbled. "'S won*nnn*derful!"

"Isn't it?" Mick demanded, climbing up onto the table and plunking down there, his sneakered feet on the seat beside Abby. He braced his elbows on his knees and put his chin in his cupped hand to watch her eat. "I get such a charge out of seeing people eat that stuff. Take a big bite. It's better that way."

Abby abandoned her manners and licked her fingers. For the moment, she forgot her starchy clothes and prim pearls and tipped her head up to the dappled sunshine and smiled at Mick Piper. "You love your work, don't you?"

"Of course. Who wouldn't?"

"How on earth did you get started?"

He shrugged as if the story was no big deal. "My uncle owned the place and I bought his shares a few years back. The Piper family owns all kinds of businesses around here, in fact—all food related."

"Your sister's bakery," Abby recalled.

"Right. And my cousin—who is actually more like a brother to me—Rob's his name. He runs a distillery. My father makes soup, and my uncle Jed makes snacks—pretzels, chips, things like that."

"If you all merged, you'd be a conglomerate yourselves."

Mick made a face. "You sound like Rob. He's always got a scheme going. No, there's no fun in conglomerates. I couldn't get excited about soup or tortilla chips. But peanut butter—that's something a man can devote his life to."

Abby laughed at him, still munching her bread and peanut butter. Perhaps it was the dazzling sunshine or the sweet taste of childhood, but she felt as if her day had taken a magical turn. A quick meeting, a silly misunderstanding, and now she was sitting with a man she felt more comfortable with than any of her current escorts. Impulsively, she said, "You're very sweet, aren't you? I mean, you're not a cut-throat businessman making money from something that little kids love."

"Oh, I make money," he cautioned, looking amused by her question. "Not enough to afford caviar at the company Christmas party, but enough."

"Even *The Epicurean* doesn't have caviar at the

Christmas party. Maybe we'd better check into canapés made with peanut butter."

He smiled, obviously enjoying himself as he watched her. Though his eyelashes were lazy, Mick Piper's gray eyes were keen and full of intelligence. He scanned Abby's face, slipping lower to appraise her shoulders, her arms and hands, and, yes, her breasts. He couldn't see below the table, so he returned his gaze to her face, looking speculative. Perhaps the sunshine had the same odd effect on him, for he hesitated momentarily. "You know," he said, more quietly this time, "I'm changing my mind about you, Dear Abby. I thought for a while there that you were a pretty stuffy snob from Chicago. You're not so bad, are you?"

Abby tried to swallow a sticky mouthful and couldn't manage.

He corrected himself. "I didn't mean that you weren't attractive before. You're just—well, I bet you drive your boyfriend crazy."

Still struggling to swallow, Abby almost choked. "I haven't got a boyfriend."

His response to that information was to smile very broadly. "No? Does that touch-me-not air of yours scare off the amateurs? I find it very appealing, Dear Abby. Sophisticated ladies have always turned me on."

"Starting with Greta?"

"Right." Joking, he added, "And ending with . . . well, you're definitely in Greta's league."

Abby met his gaze and felt time falter. Until that moment, she had understood intellectually that they were an attractive man and an attractive woman alone together, but as if the sun had come out from behind the tree branches to shed the light of reality on the situation, she

suddenly realized that Mick Piper was an attractive man
who was attracted to her, and though she'd been startled
to find an executive maverick who wore jeans and sneakers on the job, she was quite attracted to him, too. In
fact, there was a static communicative element between
them, and when Abby met Mick's eyes, a queer jolt of
understanding struck her. He had a nice smile, an en-
gaging one that no doubt drew women to him like honey
bees. It was obvious that Abby's pretended worldliness
was sparking his imagination. One false step and she
could see a very different conclusion to their interview.

Mick had seen her interest sharpen and watched as
the resulting indecision clouded her features just as swiftly.
He leaned forward. Cautiously, he reached and touched
her just under the point of her chin with his forefinger.
Perhaps he felt the tremor that rippled along her nerves,
but he didn't wait for her to object. Gently, he tipped
her face upward until the rays of sunshine warmed her
cheeks and caused her to close her eyes against the glare.

The moment stretched. The silence between them
lengthened into an intimate quiet charged with building
tension. Softly, he said, "I'll bet your lips aren't the least
bit cool."

He tipped her mouth higher, slowly, slowly descend-
ing until his lips touched hers. Abby felt something melt
inside herself just as the flavor of peanut butter had melted
on her tongue. A warm sweetness seemed to expand
within her. Mick pressed deeper, taking her mouth completely and then tilting her head until the contact was
more sensual. He was warm and firm and tasted both
sweet and slightly bitter. He smelled subtly of peanuts
and tobacco and sunshine, a delicious combination that
worked swift magic on Abby's senses. Abruptly, she was
lightheaded.

With a rhythmic nudge, Mick parted her mouth. His tongue swiped a slow, exploring stroke across her lower lip, tantalizing her with a subtle, questioning caress. He touched his tongue to hers, and Abby felt weak. Instinctively, she allowed him entry, scarcely breathing for the quick tempo of her heart. Mick wasted no time, but delved into her mouth, and savored the taste of her. Abby reached out to steady herself, laying her hand on his thigh, warm and hard beneath the denim.

His kiss was searching then, as if he had just a short time to make decisions about her. The gentleness evaporated, and he was momentarily rough, perhaps asking her to touch him some more. Abby nearly slipped her hand higher on his thigh, but she stopped herself in time. First day on the job and she was breaking rules already!

He sensed her thoughts. Slowly, regretfully, he withdrew from her until their lips were barely touching. He slipped his hand securely behind the nape of her neck, however, and held her there inescapably. He released her mouth, but stayed close, nosing the delicate line of her jaw and inhaling a long breath as if taking pleasure in the fragrance that clung to her skin. With his lips, he brushed a tender spot just below her ear.

Abby tried to draw a breath to steady her tearing heartbeat. No use. She felt weak and aroused at the same time, disconcerted by her own willingness, but foolishly longing for him to touch her. How might the gentle coupling of their mouths have changed if she'd given him a sign of encouragement? She held very still for fear she was about to sigh at the carnal sensations he had awakened.

"Hmm," he murmured against her trembling throat. "Is is too much to hope that a classy lady like you could play basketball, too?"

Abby gathered every shred of her poise. She didn't move, but forced herself to open her eyes and say composedly, "I've never been good at sports."

He sat back, releasing his hold on her but allowing his fingertips to trail regretfully back along her jawline. He smiled into her eyes, looking wicked again. "Maybe you haven't had the right coach."

They were interrupted then, and Abby didn't have a chance to respond. A car careened into the driveway, accelerating with a roar until the driver pulled even with the picnic table. Then he slammed on the brakes, and the brown Mercedes convertible slid to a noisy halt, dust flying. A man popped open the door, calling, "Mick!"

Abby sat back hastily and hoped she didn't look like a just-kissed teenager. She was thankful for the moment to compose herself.

Mick turned away from her and responded easily, "Yeah, Rob. What's up?"

Rob was Mick's cousin, Abby recalled as he shut off the car's purring engine and clambered out onto the drive, not bothering to slam the door behind himself. He was dressed in a handsome suit complete with vest and a silk handkerchief peeking from his breast pocket. His face was set into a frown. He didn't even glance at Abby. "Hell, Mick, don't you answer your telephone?"

"Not today. Judy's not back to work yet."

"You haven't heard the news."

Mick obviously saw the tension in his cousin's face, and he slid off the table at once. He automatically dusted off the seat of his jeans, asking, "What's wrong?"

"Judas, Mick, it's all over the news! Mama just heard it on the radio, and the phone's going crazy at home. The peanut butter's contaminated."

"*What?*"

Rob nodded grimly, fists cocked on his hips. "You heard me. Some bad jars have turned up in Kansas and Oklahoma, and a kid's been poisoned in Chicago. It's—"

Frozen in disbelief, Mick demanded, *"Our* peanut butter?"

"Yeah, the—"

Mick lunged and grabbed Rob's suit lapels with both hands, furious and dangerous all at once. "Dammit, Rob, you mean people have *died?"*

"No, no, no," Rob gasped, struggling in Mick's grip. "It's causing hives, swelling, and other symptoms. There may be other unreported cases, too. The peanut butter's poisoned somehow. You've got to do something, Mick. The media is screaming, and your distributors are going crazy trying to get hold of you. Mick, Mick, calm down! You've got to think and move fast."

Mick Piper slowly released his cousin's jacket. He looked stunned. And angry. He swore shortly and raked his fingers back through his hair. "Dammit, Rob, I should have known the peace wouldn't last."

CHAPTER THREE

MICK FELT AS IF he'd been eating strawberries with sweet cream one minute, and in the next minute he was hit in the stomach by a runaway Mack Truck.

It sounded silly, he knew, but Mick honestly believed that he *had* devoted most of his life to peanut butter, and if someone had purposely poisoned his product, he took the crime very personally. It hurt him physically to think his peanut butter was the cause of such a terrible catastrophe. Even Rob understood that. Rob was just a pace behind him when Mick took off at a dead run, heading for the office.

The phones were ringing like crazy already. Mick slammed into his inner office and grabbed up a receiver, and immediately the other line began to ring also. He heard Abby Vanderbine pick up the phone in the outer office, and he knew she could handle things out there.

She looked like the kind of woman with a lot of talents.

He was soon talking to the nearest FBI headquarters. With Rob breathing down his neck and offering his opinions, Mick didn't have time to think about Abby Vanderbine for the rest of the morning. He heard her on the other telephone several times, and when a station wagon full of reporters arrived outside, it was Abby who went out to speak with them. Mick was thankful for the help. He had his hands full, all right.

A news agency called, demanding a statement from Michael J. Piper about his poisonous product. Police from Oklahoma telephoned, and the Center for Disease Control wanted a line open constantly. Mick called Frank in from the plant to answer some of the chemists' more technical questions. In the early afternoon, more reporters called, this time from a Chicago television station. And so it went. The FDA called. The local state troopers arrived, complete with flashing lights and sirens, for godsake! Mick grimly listened to everyone and tried his best to answer questions.

At two o'clock, Abby Vanderbine tapped on the door and poked her head into Mick's office. She looked pretty wonderful to him right then, since he'd just slammed the phone down on a shouting physician from Atlanta. Abby was calm and self-possessed, looking as if she had just walked off the pages of *Vogue* magazine. Her crisp suit seemed like a tart lemon popsicle, sweet and cool, and her hair didn't have a wisp out of place. She was pure class and appeared utterly incongruous in his cramped and cluttered office.

"The FBI is here," she said with the quiet efficiency of an executive secretary. "They'd like to see you."

Of course the FBI was going to turn up sometime.

Mick swallowed his dismay and advanced to shake the hands of the two unsmiling agents. This was serious business, but at least they didn't have their handcuffs ready.

While Mick talked to the law-enforcement people, Rob went out to speak with Abby and the two of them drafted a short statement for the press. On the steps outside, Rob read it to the gathered reporters and did his best to answer their questions. Mick was glad to have been spared that ordeal. He took the FBI agents over to the peanut-butter plant himself to start a real investigation. They wanted to understand how the peanut butter was made, packaged, and shipped, and it took hours to go through a detailed explanation. Mick closed the plant and sent his employees home, and the FBI sealed it as a scene of a crime.

More than anyone else, Mick wanted to know how just half a dozen jars of his peanut butter had been tainted and then distributed to separate locations. The fact that there were people sick in many states was proof that either Piper's was at fault or that some kind of nationwide conspiracy was at hand.

Later that evening, after the FBI had staked out the plant and the reporters had all gone to find themselves a decent meal, Mick sat down heavily in his office chair and planted his elbows on the desk, feeling drained. He sighed and raked his hand through his hair. "Damn, I wish I knew what was going on, Rob!"

Rob grunted, thrusting his hands into the front pockets of his expensive trousers. He was the picture of an aggravated executive—complete with a roll of antacid tablets in his pocket, no doubt. Rhetorically, he said, "It's obvious that Piper's Peanut Butter is the target of someone with a bone to pick. Do you think it's a grudge against you personally, Mick?"

"Me?" Mick demanded. "I may not be a prince, but this!"

Rob was always disapproving. Even when they were kids and Rob had moved in with Mick's family after his own parents died, he had rarely been happy with what Mick did for himself. Rob thought his older cousin was too frivolous, too interested in sports and girls when intellectual pursuits should have claimed his attention. Now Rob pursed his mouth and surveyed Mick frostily from under his eyebrows. "No jealous husbands looking for a way to get some revenge?"

Mick didn't bother glorifying that question by answering it. He sent Rob a deadpan look instead.

Rob shrugged. Still frowning, he began to pace around the desk like a grouchy bear. "Well, if not with you, then someone is angry with the company, I suppose. Disgruntled employee, perhaps?"

"I can't imagine who. Relations with the labor unions are just fine."

"The police didn't have any guesses?"

"Not yet."

"I see." Rob paused, then turned on his heel to scrutinize Mick for a moment. "And they didn't . . . ask you?"

"Ask me what?"

Rob studied Mick a moment longer, as if weighing his words carefully before he spoke. Unwillingly, he said, "I can't help remembering another time when this family faced a poisoning situation, Mick."

Mick felt anger rise within himself and he glared at Rob. Until today, the past had seemed well buried. "Dammit, that was eight years ago! That's got nothing to do with this!"

"All right, all right," Rob soothed at once. "I was only thinking of possibilities, that's all."

"I'm just as shocked as you are."

"I know, I know. You don't have to assure me of anything. The FBI, though, is another story. Have they . . ."

"They haven't thought of me yet," Mick snapped. "Or maybe they have, but they're saving their questions for later."

Rob looked sorrowful, shaking his head. "The company's in bad trouble, Mick. Face it, *you're* in big trouble all over again!"

"Thanks for the information," Mick growled in annoyance. Then, relenting quickly, he said, "Forget I said that, Rob. I'm sorry. I know what kind of mess this thing is. I'd rather be sick myself than believe that something I've done has contributed to somebody else's suffering."

Abby rounded the doorway from the outer office then. She must have heard their last exchange, because she intervened. Her voice was soft, but urgent. "You shouldn't feel guilty, Mr. Piper," she said as she came in, "until you know exactly who's at fault."

Mick looked up at her, startled by her presence. He'd almost forgotten that she was there. He wondered how much she had overheard.

It was Rob who agreed with her, saying briskly, "You're right, of course, Miss Vanderbine. Mick, it can't have been your fault, so don't take this too hard, okay? *You* didn't go through a batch of peanut butter with an eye-dropper full of some kind of poisonous stuff. Do they even know what the substance was?"

"Not yet. The Center for Disease Control is working on it."

"There, you see? We shouldn't react until we know what we're dealing with. Don't get bent out of shape over something that was out of your control."

"Obviously, something *was* out of my control," Mick snapped, "because somewhere along the line I gave some nut the opportunity to—"

"Mick!" his cousin interrupted, voice harsh to quell the guilt trip.

"Your cousin is right," Abby said gently. "It's plain silly to go off the deep end until we know all the facts."

Mick glanced at her again, but did not respond. Nothing that either of them could say was going to mitigate the way he felt. He felt terrible. From the look in Abby Vanderbine's eyes, he could see that she understood the depth of his concern. Unfortunately, she was also feeling sorry for him, and Mick found her pity almost as distasteful as the thoughts of poisoned peanut butter. He wondered what her face was going to look like when the FBI started suggesting that he had tainted his own product. That thought made Mick feel even sicker.

Rob wheeled around and began to pace again, muttering, "We've got to count on the law-enforcement people for the time being. Let's hope the FBI gets this thing figured out soon—before the press eats you alive, at least. You know, this story is going to be splattered all over tomorrow's newspapers, and it won't do your peanut butter a bit of good. You'll be lucky if you can sell jars of the stuff to Third World countries after this!"

Abby hurriedly tried to cover for Rob's lack of tact, saying, "Other companies have been hit with worse disasters and survived, Mr. Piper. I'm sure that your cousin needn't worry about his company's future. No one has died!"

"Yet," Mick said dolefully.

The resulting uncomfortable silence stretched, and then

Rob must have finally realized that he was doing more harm than good. "Yes, well, don't give up the ship yet, Mick. Things will turn out okay, I'm sure. I'll run along now, I think. Miriam will be going crazy not knowing what's happened. Mick, why don't you come home with me tonight? Miriam will have something ready for dinner and—"

"No, thanks," Mick said, rousing himself to smile a little. The last thing he wanted tonight was to listen to Miriam Piper describing how she cooked pot roast or pork chops or whatever was on the menu. Honestly, he said, "I don't feel like eating, if you know what I mean. But I appreciate the offer, Rob."

"You're sure?" Rob asked, pointedly staring at his cousin, as if the power of a glare could change Mick's feelings.

Mick nodded. "I'm sure. Thanks anyway. And listen, Rob, I'm glad you came over today. I—well, it was—"

Rob nodded shortly. "Don't mention it. The rest of the family would have come today, too, but I thought the last thing we needed was a mob of relatives. We're all ready to stand by you, Mick."

Mick smiled. The family had indeed stood by him once before. He was just sorry he was going to need them again. Ruefully, he said, "Thanks. Give Miriam my love."

Rob cocked his forefinger like a pistol and winked. Then he went brusquely past Abby without a word and out into the reception area. A moment later the bell jingled and the front door crashed closed.

"Don't mind him," Mick said to Abby. "When he's got things on his mind, he's not exactly Mr. Polite."

Abby stayed at the door, one of her slim hands casually resting on the knob. She smiled and shook her head. "I didn't notice."

You didn't notice that my cousin shoved past you without acknowledging how helpful you were today? Then you've got a very thick skin, Miss Vanderbilt. We've all treated you like part of the scenery, haven't we? I'm sorry for that."

"It's Vander*bine,*" Abby corrected his unconscious mistake with a grin, "and I wouldn't let you treat me like scenery if you didn't have a good reason. Don't apologize. I know it's been a rough day."

"It would have been rougher if you hadn't been here. You were a lot of help. Thanks. You're a real pro when it comes to handling the press, aren't you?"

"As a matter of fact, I used to be a newspaper reporter. I'm good at fending off the press now because I've been fended off myself by some real experts!"

"I guess you're still a reporter, aren't you?" he asked vaguely, squinting a little as he tried to concentrate. It had been a rough day, all right. He could hardly think, and frankly he didn't want to have to think too hard. All he really wanted to do was to look at a lovely young woman and forget about what had happened.

She looked almost regal, Mick decided as he gazed at her. She looked classy and elegant and *rich.* It wasn't just her clothes, which probably had French or Italian labels sewn inside, but it was her composure, he decided thoughtfully. She was a genteel young woman, too slender to be totally queenlike, and yet she had a kind of unbreakable strength about her—a slim but flexible sort of female strength. Beneath her starchy suit and neatly pressed cotton blouse, her body gave away more clues to her personality. She was made up of curves, not straight lines and sharp angles. She was long-legged and probably tall for a woman, though next to him she seemed small. Her graceful walk and delicate waistline made Mick think of expensive Siamese cats. Yes, with her sandy-white blond hair, those thick black lashes, and very blue, almost slanted eyes, she did remind him of a cat. Her mouth, though full and delicious, had a slightly short upper lip, a clever kitten's mouth.

Suddenly, Mick didn't want to think about peanut butter anymore. He didn't want to remember a single detail of the day. He wanted to lose himself in this gracious young woman instead. She looked so out of place just then that she might have arrived from an exotic foreign capital, and that fit Mick's mood perfectly. Blue Creek, West Virginia, didn't grow women like this one, and he had never wanted to be so far from Blue Creek in his life. He wondered what Abby Vanderbine's hair might look like if it was loosened from that sophisticated little twist. How might it feel between his fingers? How might that lovely, slender body feel under his hands?

He collected himself abruptly before he got carried away. What an idiot he could be! He didn't have a prayer with the polished likes of Miss Abigail Vanderbine. She looked like the type who might marry a senator and someday be the mother of a President. Or maybe she would become the matriarch of some fabulously wealthy perfume dynasty. Mick shook his head. He was definitely out of his league with this one now. Maybe once he could have matched her, but certainly not anymore. He'd been hiding in Blue Creek too long. He might as well forget about an idyllic evening with this blue-blooded female.

Trying to be pleasant, though, he remarked, "After

everything today, I almost forgot you came from that magazine. You're getting a hell of a story, aren't you?"

Abby smiled and approached the desk with purposeful steps. "I can see that you're so tired you can hardly make pointless conversation. Why don't you go home, Mr. Piper? You'd better get some sleep and something nourishing to eat. This is going to be a long haul, you know. Come on."

She laid her hands on the arms of his chair and spun him away from the desk, bending close. She smelled absolutely fabulous—not so musky as he was afraid she might. Mick fleetingly thought a man could painlessly drown in a subtle fragrance like hers. He smiled, too, for like a mother hen, she took his shirt by the sleeve and drew him to his feet.

He obeyed her, of course, but inquired, "Are you taking care of me, Miss Vanderbine?"

Abby guided him gently around the desk and headed for the doorway. "You could use some good care, considering the day you've had. Think of me as a Good Samaritan."

"Or the Lone Ranger," he said without thinking. He heard himself ask wistfully, "Are you going to ride off into the sunset on your horse when you're finished?"

Abby laughed and said, "No, I'm going to have to settle for a rental car, I'm afraid."

He stopped at once, and reality flooded into his brain. "Hey, you're not planning on driving back tonight to— to—where are you from, anyway? Judas, I don't know a thing about you!"

"I'm living in Chicago," Abby explained swiftly to allay his concern. "That's where the magazine offices are, anyway. I'm only driving as far as Charleston, though, and I can catch a plane for—"

"You can't drive the whole way to Charleston tonight!" Mick objected, feeling foolish for having enjoyed a moment's pleasant reverie when she had such a long night ahead of her. "It's two hours, and you've been just as busy as the rest of us!"

Abby snapped off the lights in his office and then picked up the linen jacket of her suit. She hesitated and looked sideways at Mick. "Does this town have a hotel?"

"Are you kidding?" Mick asked, feeling relief. She wanted to stay, after all. She wasn't going to try driving back to the airport tonight. All he needed on top of everything else was to be the cause of an exhausted woman's automobile accident! With a grin, he said, "This town doesn't even have a bar, let alone a motel. On the other hand, I think we can find a place for you to stay overnight."

The words were out of his mouth before he'd even thought them through carefully, but suddenly he wanted nothing more than to spend the whole night with this lovely lady. She was cool and possessed, but there was something else even more appealing about her. He'd seen it in the moment she had hesitated, the moment she gave away the fact that she *was* tired and would like to avoid a long drive. Perhaps she wasn't as sophisticated as she looked.

Yes, Mick thought abruptly. He'd seen it this morning, too. They had been sitting outside under the apple trees and he'd seen her face change. Her features softened, her eyes had warmed, and she'd been *younger* somehow, gentler, perhaps, more fun. He'd seen a glimpse of a different woman inside the crisp package she presented to the world. With a funny flash of recognition, Mick decided that Abby Vanderbine was like a little girl playing in her big sister's clothes. The look in her eyes had given her away. She was a sentimental romantic, and that had prompted Mick to kiss her once already.

Now, he wanted to kiss her again. He wanted to forget the rest of the world and spend the whole night getting to know the misty-eyed girl he'd discovered that morning. It had been a long time since he'd felt urges like that.

Before he had even thought things through completely, he took three strides and reached for her equipment case. "If you're not too fussy, you can stay at my place," he said.

"Your place?" she repeated.

He couldn't help smiling at her expression, and he remembered how startled she'd looked after he had kissed her that morning. He said, "You're blushing again. That's really very attractive in a lady like yourself. Look, I realize that a little West Virginia town is not your cup of tea exactly, and you didn't mean to get so involved today, but it would be really irresponsible of me to let you drive all the way to the airport tonight. I insist you stay. The alternative to my place is my mother's house, I suppose, but between you and me, I'd think twice before agreeing to spending the night under her roof."

"Why?"

Mick lifted the bag and said, "I might be a charity case at the moment, but my mother will draft you into working for some cause that you can't walk away from tomorrow morning. She's a philanthropic terror. What do you say?"

"About staying with her?" Abby asked, looking composed. "Or with you?"

"With me," Mick replied, and he held her eyes again. He wanted to convince her, to thaw her out just a little more. He was practically aching inside, he wanted her so much. She was lovely. And how did a woman develop so many interesting nooks and crannies? There was a hollow at the base of her throat that he wanted very much to touch. Behind her ears—yes, he remembered vaguely the sweet scent of her there and how dry and warm her velvety skin had felt against his lips. And just under her breast—he could hardly see it through her unbuttoned jacket, but he was sure he'd caught a glimpse of a feminine shadow there, just the kind of warm spot a man liked to explore with great care.

She looked doubtful beneath her cool exterior, however. She didn't trust him, maybe. Or perhaps—if he was lucky—she didn't trust herself.

Coaxing, he said, "I'm pretty tame."

"Are you?" she asked, lifting her eyebrows delicately.

He smiled a little more, having heard her wary tone. "Well, I'll warn you in advance that soft candles and blond women in pink nightgowns turn me into a crazy man, but if you've been lucky enough to bring along blue pajamas or something instead, I think we're safe for one night at least."

She blushed then, and the sight of her warming cheeks was more than Mick could stand. He almost dropped the case and grabbed her right then and there with a noisy groan of pure animal satisfaction. He wanted to bury his mouth in her satin-smooth skin and breathe the intoxicating scent of her. He wanted to taste her lips again and nudge that pearl necklace aside to savor the softness of her throat. He wanted to pick her up and cuddle her fragile body next to his.

But he didn't. He would have made a fool of himself, of course. She'd probably scream. Or maybe faint. With a flash of insight, Mick was wryly reminded of that big, clumsy Walt Disney dog that was always acting stupid. What was his name? Goofy, that was it. *Goofy Makes Love to Snow White.* It would be one hilarious movie, all right. Goofy in his big sneakers and flannel shirt, and Snow White looking virginal in pale-yellow linen.

Chagrined by that mental image, he said, "Listen, I can't ask you to stay after all the help you've been today. But if you take it easy tonight, maybe by morning you'll feel strong enough to—"

"I'm stronger than you think," she interrupted quietly. "I wouldn't have stayed today if I hadn't wanted to."

"Oh," he said, taken so thoroughly aback by that response that he must have looked stupidly blank. Goofy, indeed! "Well, if—"

"What I mean," she said carefully, "is that I felt I could help, and you needed it. I walked away from a— a situation a little like this once before, and I haven't forgiven myself since."

"What d'you mean?" Mick asked, curious at once.

"Well, it's a long story," she said, giving him an apologetic smile and lifting her luminous blue eyes to his. "It doesn't matter, really. I shouldn't have said that, but—"

"I'd like to hear the story," he coaxed.

She shook her head swiftly, demurely, and avoided looking at him. "It was—oh, I was a reporter in Chicago, before I started writing for *The Epicurean,* and I had been working on a local news story there about a—a disreputable appliance-store owner. I'm sorry, I didn't mean to imply that you're a disreputable anything—"

"Go on," he said. "What about him?"

"Well," she said, apparently wishing she hadn't brought up the subject, "my partner and I worked on the story

for months. We exposed this man's bad business prac-
tices, and I—well, we drove him out of business, quite
frankly."

Mick managed a smile. "You won't drive me out of
business, you know."

"Of course not," she said, looking up at him. Her
blue eyes were filled with a volatile emotion he couldn't
name. Pain? Regret? Mick felt a hot rush of sympathy
for her. Haltingly, she said, "I wish that had been the
end of the story. I had become acquainted with the store
owner, you see. He wasn't really a bad person, he was
just—well, looking for easy answers, I guess. He had
a difficult time after our story and—" She sighed sharply
and said, "After several months, you see, he shot himself."

"Good God," Mick breathed, watching as her eyes
began to glisten. Whatever feelings of lust he'd just had
for this woman drained away in a split second. He wanted
to take her in his arms and comfort her.

"I couldn't help feeling terribly guilty," she explained
in a rush. "Maybe I could have done something, you
know? It was—well, I have such terrible second thoughts
now when I walk away from a difficult situation. Today
I couldn't help thinking . . ."

"I see."

"No, you don't," she said firmly. "I don't think you're
the suicidal type, but—"

"Thanks for that much," he said dryly.

"But I—I thought I could be helpful today. I won't
stay and watch over you like a guardian angel, of course.
I don't pretend I can be that significant. I just didn't want
to leave when my own memories were so—so strong.
Do you understand?"

Her face was turned up to his and looked positively

ethereal in the evening light. Her eyes were lovely, and her black lashes were sparkling with contained tears. Her mouth, again, looked soft and unspeakably delicious.

Mick withheld a sigh. Well, he had just been reduced to a charity case. He'd been conjuring up all sorts of erotic scenarios involving this ladylike creature, and all along she had pigeonholed him in the same category as abandoned orphans and stray puppies! Some days were a dead loss all around, he supposed. This was definitely not one of the most memorable days in the life of Michael J. Piper.

However, he decided, taking yet another thoughtful look at Abby Vanderbine, some orphans and puppies got very good treatment, indeed.

CHAPTER FOUR

ABBY ENDED UP DRIVING, for she discovered that Mick Piper usually rode his bicycle back and forth to work every day. When she was in the car with him, hands on the wheel and eyes on the road, she had time to feel foolish. Why had she told him about that wretched business in Chicago? The circumstances of Jerry Freytag's death probably sounded stupid to a vital, energetic man like Mick. And she had almost cried, too! That would really have given away her lack of sophistication.

At least she hadn't blurted out the portion of the story concerning Ryan O'Shea, her partner on the local business beat. Ryan had laughed at her emotional reaction to Jerry Freytag's suicide. He had lectured her, too.

"You've got to get tough in this game, Abs," he'd chided her. He had tossed aside the obituary with a shrug. "Don't let it bother you. It wasn't our fault, y'know."

But it *had* bothered Abby. She'd decided to quit working for the paper, because she wasn't tough enough to handle the cut-throat side of journalism. Working for *The Epicurean* was more her speed—easy interviews and recipes and no breakneck deadlines. And she decided to move out of Ryan's apartment, too. She and Ryan were no longer the happy lovers they had once been. They had been attracted to one another on the job, and the feeling had led to a heated romance. The romance hadn't lasted, though. Either Ryan had changed, or Abby's perspective on his personality had shifted. Abby knew it was time to start all over again for herself. Oddly enough, Ryan hadn't seemed too upset when she told him of her decisions.

"Okay," he'd said with that same maddeningly casual tone that Abby had found increasingly exasperating. "I guess I'll see you around."

Abby brushed aside her memory of Ryan and glanced across the darkened front seat of the car at Mick Piper. *He* wasn't the type to suppress his anxiety into some kind of macho-smooth act. At that moment, he was frowning. Though his long legs were relaxed, he had one elbow braced against the window and was running his hand back through his hair, thinking. He had a lot on his mind, she was sure. He certainly didn't need the added complication of a silly woman on his hands. Once again, Abby felt sorry for him.

"Listen," she said, interrupting his thoughts as gently as possible, "maybe I ought to just drop you off and find someplace to go."

He sat up straighter in the passenger seat and said, "No, no. I'd feel terrible if you did. I mean—as long as you don't have your hopes up about the accommodations. I'm not known for my housekeeping, so—"

"Please don't start making excuses," Abby said, smiling at him as she drove. "You must think I stay at the Hilton everywhere I travel!"

"Don't you?" he asked, sounding surprised.

"Not everywhere," Abby shot back haughtily, enjoying teasing him. She watched the road and drove carefully. "I have to set a good example for the rest of the staff, you see."

"Why?"

"My father publishes *The Epicurean*." She glanced at him again to see his reaction to that information, but his face was in shadow. Abby interpreted his silence as disapproval, which she was accustomed to, though she really didn't want it from Mick Piper. "Yes," she said when he didn't respond, "I was hired purely as an act of nepotism, and I make no apologies. I pull my weight. My father is like General Patton, you see. He eats what the rest of the soldiers eat, and so must the rest of the family. I stay wherever I can get a room."

"I see," Mick said, apparently digesting the information that she was the daughter of a magazine publisher. "Uh, turn here. See the mailbox? Say, maybe we'd better find somebody to drive you to the airport after all. My place isn't going to be up to your standards, I can tell." Almost in an undertone, he added, "Unless you like sawdust."

"Sawdust?"

"Yeah, I'm still—well, the house isn't finished yet. I don't mind roughing it, but you're different."

"Nonsense." Abby pulled up in front of a closed garage door and set the parking brake. "Now I'm intrigued. You're going to have to at least show me the place."

"Well, I had to give my key to the guy from the FBI. They were going to have a look around today."

"I'm sure they tidied up after themselves."

Mick smiled ruefully at that and reached to open his door. "I thought I could blame the mess on them. Oh, well. Okay, Dear Abby. This way."

He carried her case along a flagstone walkway, and Abby hung back to take a look at her surroundings. The meager moonlight illuminated a half-hearted attempt at a lawn that was bisected by what appeared to be a small creek that widened into a pond. She could see the swaying stalks of cattails near the water. There were beech trees by the dozen, clustered into three groups and surrounded by lush, ground-hugging bushes. The landscape looked natural, not planted by experts, and yet it was appealing to the eye.

Most interesting of all was the house, a stark, geometrical structure built of cedar and nestled into the trees for privacy from the road. The entrance to the house was sheltered by a tall archway, through which they passed before being confronted by a set of double doors made of unpainted oak. Mick unlocked one door and pushed it wide for Abby. When she stepped inside cautiously, he said, "Don't be scared. He's not real."

"He" turned out to be a human-sized statue of Mr. Peanut, complete with top hat and monocle, who was standing just inside the doorway of the house. Abby choked down a gasp and began to laugh once she realized the tall statue wasn't alive. A baseball cap had been slung on Mr. Peanut's walking stick, and a tweed jacket was hanging from one outstretched and gloved hand. Mr. Peanut had been relegated to coat-rack duty.

When Mick closed the door and flipped on a light, Abby could see that the statue was not the only whimsical touch in his house. The lamp over their heads was a pounded-tin fixture reminiscent of days gone by, imprinted with a pattern of ducklings chasing one another. The floorboards beneath their feet were smooth and polished, but a parade of stenciled peanuts rolled in a never-ending line around the baseboards.

"How lovely!" Abby breathed, meaning it. Without an invitation, she went up the three steps to the landing of the house and looked into a long, bare-floored sitting room. The light from the entrance spilled along the floor and threw the huge stones of a fireplace into dramatic relief. There wasn't much furniture. Just a low sofa and one wing chair stood near the dark fireplace, with some occasional tables and a brass floor lamp.

"They didn't tear the place apart at least," Mick noted.

"It's charming!"

"This part of the house is finished," Mick explained, coming up the steps behind her. "The trail of sawdust doesn't start until you head back toward the bedrooms. The kitchen is that way—in the original plans it was called a keeping room, so it's big and I don't have much occasion to use this room. I've never bothered with a lot of furniture out here."

"Goodness, but this is a big place!" Abby said, looking around. "Much bigger than it looks from the outside."

"It does echo sometimes," Mick admitted. He went past her and kept going in the direction of the kitchen. His sneakered footsteps were indeed amplified by the emptiness of the rooms.

Abby followed him slowly, taking note of the house. It was just as stark on the inside as it was out, and that surprised her. She expected a much different kind of home for Mick Piper.

The kitchen set her straight, however. It was a clut-

tered, homey room with an arched, beamed ceiling and
a mismatch of furniture that looked comfortable and well-
used. There were no signs of a violent police search.

The long room was divided into three areas: a cooking
work area complete with the kind of islands seen in
decorating magazines; a denlike corner with another fireplace, a lumpy sofa, magazine rack, and footstool; and
a breakfast nook with a Tiffany-style lamp, a round ped-
estal table, and three captain's chairs. Unlike the echoing
living room, there were pictures on the walls here—a
landscape of a Mail Pouch barn, a photograph of pine
trees and grazing cattle, and—oddly—a museum poster
for a Manet show at the Metropolitan. There was a cork
bulletin board, too, with messages and Polaroid photos
pinned haphazardly around a cartoon drawing of a beleaguered Snoopy who had apparently been struck on the
head by a basketball. The ball was pictured, and there
were dizzy rings drawn around Snoopy's discombobu-
lated head.

"The housekeeper comes on Tuesdays," Mick said,
looking around at the clutter as if wishing it might disappear into a puff of magic smoke. "I'm afraid this is a
bad reflection on my character, isn't it?"

On the contrary, the sight of the slightly cluttered room
made Abby feel like kicking off her shoes and diving
for the sofa. With a cup of hot chocolate or even a beer,
she would be more than content. She could even imagine
curling up with a man like Mick Piper right there on
those calico cushions for a drowsy conversation while
she unbuttoned that soft shirt of his and—

No, no, no! Abby remembered herself abruptly. Mick
Piper believed that she was a class act, too poised to
behave like a hoyden or a cavewoman. He had kissed

her because he liked sophisticated ladies, and for some reason Abby wanted Mick to go on liking her. She wanted him to look at her the way he had that morning before all the commotion started. She *liked* Mick Piper, she decided. Not just because he appeared to be a nice guy, but because he was a perfectly available, wonderfully attractive, and sexy man.

She would have to go on playing the role of Abigail Vanderbine, that was all.

As she stood in the entrance of his humble but homey kitchen, Abby decided that she wanted to get to know Mick as quickly and as thoroughly as possible. And the way to keep him interested in her was to act like a lady. What had he called it? Her touch-me-not air? That was it. Be cool and poised, Abby dear. You can occasionally catch bees with refrigerated honey, she thought. It just depends on the bee. It was obvious that Mick Piper liked his women as sophisticated as possible.

So instead of flinging herself onto his sofa, she decided to collect herself before giving away her act. Mustering the cool voice her mother often used, Abby said, "I think it's charming."

"Hmm," Mick said, sounding unconvinced. He set her equipment case on the island counter and asked, "Would you like something to eat? I'm not stocked for anything fancy, but there's bound to be eggs and cheese, at least."

"No peanut butter?"

"For once," Mick said grimly, "I don't even want to smell peanut butter."

"Of course," Abby said hastily, abandoning her dreams of seduction and feeling sorry she had reminded him of the day's misfortune.

"How about you?" Mick asked. "Hungry?"

Did real ladies ever get hungry? she asked herself. Her stomach was almost growling from lack of food, but Abby remembered *Gone With the Wind* and Mammy urging Scarlet to eat a big supper before she went to the barbeque so her beaux would think she ate like a sparrow. No, Abby thought, real ladies did not feel hunger. She ignored the voice of common sense shrieking in the back of her head and said, "I'm not very hungry, to tell the truth. Just a little tired. Perhaps a cup of tea would revive me."

"Oh. Okay." Mick crossed to the cupboards and began to rifle through them, saying, "Tea, tea. There's bound to be some. Let me look around a little . . ."

They were interrupted by the arrival of a cat. It slipped around the doorway and brushed against Abby's legs, so she jumped and bit back a squeal of surprise.

Pleased with itself, the marmalade cat leaped to the top of the counter and sat down, smiling with satisfaction at having caused Abby to jump out of her skin. He lashed his tail and stared at her, positively grinning.

"Did he scare you?" Mick asked at once. "He's always doing that to strangers. He's the affectionate kind, though. He won't scratch."

"Even affection can take a person by surprise. Goodness, he looks smug, doesn't he?" Abby, a cat lover from way back, made a beeline for the animal and caught him up in her arms before he could escape. He was a big cat, fat around the middle and with a nick bitten out of his ear. She played with him smiling. "What's your name, big boy? You look like Marlon Brando—beaten-up and overweight."

"His name is Jelly," Mick said. "Ah, the teabags!"

"Jelly?" Abby asked, laughing as she cuddled the beast. "I should have guessed!" She captured his front paws in one hand and rolled the cat onto his back in her arm like a baby.

She played with the placid cat, but stole a look at her host. Mick was rummaging through his cupboards in search of some cups, his back turned to her. He looked very tall just then, and his shoulders looked nicely firm under his shirt. His worn jeans clung casually to his hips, riding a little low on the muscle of his lower back. Very nice, Abby thought. Reporters didn't have bodies like that, and neither did desk-bound executives. Mick's strong frame made her think of those mythical West Virginia mountain men—unconventional and a little uncivilized, perhaps, but with their own unique code of honor. Abby wondered how womenfolk might fit into this particular man's code. Why was he so attracted to Greta Garbo types? Was it simply a case of opposites attract?

Puzzling, Abby kneaded Jelly's stomach. Longing to ask Mick a hundred too-intimate questions, she said playfully to the cat, "I'll bet you're a rascal, aren't you, Jelly?"

"He's a terror," Mick said. He put a cup on the counter and reached for the kettle.

Jelly smiled languidly up at Abby as if agreeing wholeheartedly with Mick's assessment of his character. He began to purr as she rubbed his tummy. "Are you a terror?" Abby asked, nuzzling the cat's fur with her nose. "I'll bet you chase all the lady cats around and around, don't you, Jelly? Are you a ladies' man?"

"He's not," Mick said, puttering at the stove. "There isn't another cat for miles except one wild female that lives in the garage. She gives him a hard time, but he seems to enjoy it and doesn't stray. Either he's the world's first monogamous cat, or he's too lazy to go looking for more girl friends."

Abby rubbed Jelly's fat tummy and said boldly, "I admire a man who's loyal, Jelly. Good for you. I wonder if your master is just as well behaved?"

Mick laughed and turned away from the stove. He leaned his hip there and watched Abby play with his cat, arms folded across his chest. He shook his head. "I'm not much of a skirt-chaser, either, to tell you the truth."

"No?" Abby asked, looking up at him with a smile. She was exploring uneasy ground, but decided it was safe enough to say, "I'd have guessed you'd be a very popular man, Mr. Piper."

"Since you're moving in for the night, you'd better call me Mick," he said lightly, a smile playing on his mouth as he watched her handle his pet. After the smallest hesitation, he answered her question. "I'm not all that popular, to be honest. I'm like Jelly, I guess. I stick to my business or stay at home and work on the house." Then, abruptly, he said, "I'm a widower."

Abby stopped herself from staring and said, "Oh, I see."

"My wife died several years ago," Mick explained, turning back to the stove and laying his hand on the tea kettle to judge how quickly it was heating up. It was a nervous gesture, or perhaps he was just giving Abby time to digest the facts. Not looking at her, he said, "When she died, I moved back here to Blue Creek. After a while I started building this house to give myself something to—well, I never quite finished it, as you can see. I keep plenty busy, but I don't hang out at the local version of a singles bar."

"I see," Abby said again, feeling bad that she'd pressed him for details. She hadn't meant to get into a discussion about his love life, and she had certainly opened a larger can of worms. Inadequately, she said, "I'm sorry you've been alone."

He shrugged. "I'm not really alone. I—well, today you got a sample of how protective my family is, the way Rob came roaring to my rescue at the first sign of trouble. And I do have a lot of friends here."

"Not any children, though?"

"No. Laura was just twenty-one when we got married, and I was only two years out of college. She got sick about a year later, so we didn't have time to *think* about kids, let alone—" He stopped again. Then, as if answering a question he was sure was about to come, he said, "She had cancer."

"Oh, I'm sorry," Abby said, feeling genuine sorrow for so young a couple. She couldn't imagine a big, vibrant man with Mick's *joie de vivre* being faced with such a terrible trauma. Bad things like cancer weren't supposed to happen to young people like him. She stopped cuddling Jelly and set the cat on his feet on the counter. "It must have been very difficult."

He shrugged. "You have to take the cards you're dealt."

Abby didn't respond right away. Mick was thinking, she could see. He wanted to tell her more, perhaps. Or maybe he was uneasy about something. She couldn't be sure.

He lifted a cup from a rack, set it on the stove, and then proceeded to toy with the handle. He kept his head bent. "It was difficult," he said after a moment. "And I think it's going to get difficult again. By tomorrow, they'll have figured it out."

Abby wasn't sure she had heard correctly. "Figured what out?"

"My wife," Mick said slowly, "was very sick. She was afraid of the sickness, though. Terrified by what it was going to do to her. I think she didn't want to—to go through everything the doctors told her about. She took some pills."

"Oh," was all Abby could say. Mick Piper's wife had killed herself.

The tea kettle began to hiss, and in an instant, the whistle began. Mick removed the kettle from the heat, saying, "When Laura died, nobody except her doctor and I knew how sick she was—not even her parents. Nobody could understand why she had done such a thing to herself."

"That's understandable."

Mick shook his head. He poured boiling water into the waiting cup. "I mean they *really* didn't believe she had done it to herself. Some people thought that I had poisoned her."

"You?"

He botched the job of dunking the teabag into the cup and splashed water on the counter. "It was a mistake, of course. Things looked bad for me because Laura and I hadn't been getting along for a while—neither of us coped with her illness very well. So when she died, they thought that I had—"

"No!"

"That I had killed her," he finished. Then, rapidly, he explained, "I only sat in jail for a few days, but it was—it's funny about being innocent until you're proven guilty. A lot of people thought I *had* poisoned my wife and I'd gotten off the hook somehow. I was working in Los

Angeles for an investment firm. Even my boss still believed that I was the villain in the whole mess. I felt as though my life was pretty messed up by that time, anyway, so I came back to Blue Creek."

"And now this. The poisoning of the peanut butter."

"Yes," Mick said, and he let out a long breath. "Some bright cop is going to remember about Laura pretty soon. No matter how it happened, I might get the blame for this poisoning."

"You can't believe that you'd become a suspect simply because of— Wait, did you stand trial for your wife's death?"

"I wasn't even arraigned," he said calmly. "I just sat in jail until they got all the facts put together and decided they'd made a mistake about me."

Appalled by the thoughts of a young man grieving for his wife in the cold confines of a jail cell, Abby said swiftly, "Surely that won't matter now!"

Mick set the spoon on the counter and sent Abby a look. "You're a reporter. Wouldn't my past be an interesting tidbit to add to an article?"

He was right, of course. The newspapers were going to love this new angle to the story. PEANUT BUTTER MANUFACTURER POISONED HIS OWN WIFE. It didn't matter if Mick had never been tried for the crime. Just the fact that he'd been under suspicion was enough to titillate the public interest. It was the kind of story that sold a lot of newspapers.

But a cooler part of Abby reasoned that there must have been some reason for the police to clap him behind bars while they finished their investigation. There must have been some kind of evidence, which Mick hadn't mentioned.

Why would they arrest him, if they hadn't been sure he was guilty? And newspapers didn't print stories without justification. Perhaps Mick hadn't told her everything yet. After all, she had known him only half a day.

Abby watched Mick take the spoon from the counter, wondering about him. In his big hand, the spoon seemed remarkably small and delicate. He was a strong man, no doubt. How well did she know him, after all? Hadn't she agreed to come spend the night under his roof a little prematurely? Had she let one kiss influence her thinking so thoroughly that she was taking chances? Mick's kiss had seemed so spontaneous, so sensual, and so full of energy that it had taken her by storm. He had charmed her, pure and simple.

Was the man who made her head spin this morning capable of poisoning his own wife?

Mick finished making the tea and tapped the spoon on the edge of the cup three times. He laid the spoon aside and picked up the drink. He turned toward Abby. With one hand he held the steaming tea to her.

"Here," he said. "Maybe this will revive you. Would you like some sugar?"

CHAPTER FIVE

ABBY FORCED HERSELF to take the cup from his hand. Without even pausing to think about how hot the tea was going to be, she took a big slurp and nearly scalded the inside of her mouth.

Mick was smiling. "Thanks," he said. "That was a nice vote of confidence."

Her eyes were watering, and she could hardly summon her voice. Trying to make a joke, she gasped, "There are people who know that I've come here."

He laughed and crossed to the refrigerator. "You're safe enough without that threat."

"Unless I brought a pink nightgown, right?"

"Did you?" he asked, pausing in the act of opening the refrigerator door. His gray eyes were suddenly direct and his smile looked different somehow.

"No," Abby said, regaining her poise altogether. "As

a matter of fact, I didn't bring much of anything. I expected to go back to Chicago today, or if need be spend one night at a hotel near the Charleston airport. I travel very light."

"Maybe that's good news," Mick said slowly.

Abby heard his tone and realized that the evening could go in several directions.

Face it, she said to herself. If she really lost her head, she could end up sleeping with Mick Piper! The prospect didn't shock Abby. In fact, under different circumstances she might have welcomed a night with a man as pleasant and honest as Mick. But even though she had felt a warm rapport growing between them from the moment they met, Abby had to acknowledge that she had only known the man a few hours. She wasn't the kind of woman who could shed her clothes and her strict upbringing as easily as that.

She didn't want to hurt his feelings, though. And, crazy as it seemed, she wasn't sure she wanted to discourage Mick completely, either. As he reached into the refrigerator for a can of beer, Abby chose her words with care. "I'm afraid that if you want to see the alternative to that pink nightie, you're definitely going to have to slip something into my tea."

He glanced up. "How do you know I haven't?"

"You haven't," Abby said firmly, holding the hot cup with both her hands. Her momentary unease about accepting tea from him had evaporated. "Any man who makes peanut butter his life's work would never stoop to tactics like that."

"You trust me, don't you?" he asked, sounding surprised. He closed the door quietly and remained there, watching her.

"Is there any reason why I shouldn't?"

"Most people don't," Mick admitted, and he glanced down at the beer in his hand. "Especially after they've heard about—"

"Look," Abby intervened gently, "maybe I'm the gullible sort, but I think you're a nice man. And I wouldn't have come here tonight if I thought your motives are anything but honorable."

Mick shook his head and grinned. "So now I can't switch techniques, can I?" He popped the top on the beer can, looked at her, and said bluntly, "Believe me, Dear Abby, my thoughts are anything but honorable."

She smiled, tipping her head. "I'm flattered."

"Will you at least tell me what color your nightgown is?"

"For the sake of how well both of us sleep tonight," Abby said lightly, "I think I'll keep it a secret."

He laughed and suggested that they sit down at the table together for a while. Seeing his ingenuous smile again, Abby willingly obeyed. She sat with him and drank her tea, gathering more impressions of the man as he talked with her. Mick was unique, she thought. A combination of nice guy and something else she couldn't put her finger on yet. Was he dangerous? She didn't think so.

Mick got himself a box of crackers and some cheese. He ate his snack and talked aimlessly, but pleasantly. Supposedly for the purpose of her article, he told her a little about the peanut-butter business, but that didn't last. Obviously, Mick didn't want to be reminded of what had happened that day. Under Abby's gentle guidance, the conversation gradually wound its way to his family and their respective businesses. Abby found herself listening to every word and watching Mick's expressions. His smile was quick, and his gray eyes were expressive—one minute filled with lamplight and laughter, the next dark and solemn when some remark reminded him of his poisoned peanut butter. Abby hastened to keep the conversation light and steered it away from what had happened that day.

After a time, he came to tell her about Rob Piper's distillery, a company that made a pretty fair blend of bourbon, Mick said. Rob had tagged on Mick's heels as a kid.

"But now he thinks I'm no good," Mick reported. "I'm not an aggressive capitalist like he is."

"He makes bourbon to make money, is that it?"

"Exactly. The bad news is that he's not doing very well. The American bourbon market is not good right now, and Rob is losing money, much to his chagrin. If I were making piles, he'd really be depressed."

"Why is he so worried about what you do?"

Mick shrugged. "It's always been that way. It's a weird relationship, I know. We care about each other, but deep down, I think we're very hot competitors. From high-school grades and girls to—well, to the work we're doing now. Rob doesn't want to be left behind, and I—well, I've been very lucky all my life."

Abby thought of Laura Piper, but she did not speak.

"Anyway," Mick went on, "my relationship with Rob goes back a long way. His folks—my aunt and uncle—died when he was about eight. He came to live with us. He and I shared a room, and he even began to call my parents Mom and Dad. He's a year younger than I am, but we've been like twin brothers since then. Except that Rob kind of went off the deep end when he got to college.

The classes in economics went to his head, I guess."

"Not to yours?"

"Oh, sure," Mick said offhandedly. "I was an okay student. I'm a pretty fair businessman, too, if I don't say so myself. But Rob, well, he's highly motivated."

"You mean highly competitive. Competing with *you.*"

Mick laughed. "That sounds silly, doesn't it? Two grown men. But—well, there was a time . . ."

"Cars and girls and a position on the football team?" Abby guessed, amused.

Mick grinned at her and looked away. "Yes, all those things. Why, even Laura—Rob introduced me to her, you see. She was in his class in school, and he had a terrific crush on her. But she and I clicked, and Rob drifted off."

"So now he's going to prove that he's a better man than you are, right? A better businessman, at least."

"Maybe. And maybe he's right. I'm not as aggressive as Rob is," Mick admitted. "I'm too satisfied with the way things are—were. Rob is always looking for new ways to make money. He wants to buy some shares in the peanut-butter company so he can force me to start making millions, I think."

"You don't own Piper's Peanut Butter?" Abby asked, absently helping herself to a wedge of his cheese.

"Not all of it. I own thirty percent of the shares, but the rest is owned by stockholders. Members of my family make up most of the stockholders. Very incestuous."

"At least you know everybody. Big business doesn't always work that way."

Mick smiled a little and drank his beer. "You're right. I've already done my time in big business, and I don't want to go back."

Abby resisted the temptation to ask him about his business experience. With a flash of insight, she asked, "Would you rather own the company yourself?"

"I'm trying to. Whenever some shares come up for sale, I try to buy them. It's an expensive and slow way to gain ownership, though. I keep thinking that some year at Christmas we should all just give each other our own companies. More cheese?"

With her mouth full, Abby shook her head.

Mick began to wrap up the leftovers. Musing, he said, "I guess the whole issue of owning the company myself could be settled pretty soon, if I have to close down Piper's Peanut Butter."

"Do you really think that's a possibility?" Abby asked after she had swallowed. She stayed in her chair and watched while Mick got up and went to the refrigerator again.

"Sure, it's a possibility. Every consumer in America is going to throw away the jar of Piper's they've got in their cupboards, and it's going to take months to regain public confidence. Even if we discover that my company is perfectly innocent, it's going to be very tough recovering. I'll bet all the stockholders will be begging me to buy their shares pretty soon."

Abby smiled up at him. "You can always hope."

He grinned, nodding. "I guess so. Listen, you must be beat. Ready for bed?"

Abby was surprised to see by her watch that it was nearly midnight. "Yes, I guess I am. I'm usually a night owl, but after today . . ."

"I know what you mean. Come with me and I'll show you the presidential suite."

Quite without the awkwardness Abby expected, Mick

led her back through a darkened hallway and up a half dozen steps. She couldn't see where she was going, but she sensed that the space they entered was large. It was cooler there, and their footsteps echoed eerily. The smell of sawdust was thick.

"I'm pretty neat with the tools," Mick was saying, "but occasionally I leave something lying around, so watch where you step. This bathroom's in working order. Here's the switch."

He finally flicked on a light, and Abby took a look around. The bedroom wing of the house was barely finished at all. There were no walls, just lines of studs that outlined where the rooms were supposed to be. Fortunately, the bathroom did have walls and even a door, but beyond that, the place was spacious and a little scary.

"I told you it wasn't the Hilton," Mick said. "Here's the bed. You're welcome to hang your clothes in the closet. That's the closet there—no doors yet. I'm roughing it."

"I guess you don't really need them, do you?" Abby asked. "This place is going to be pretty spectacular when it's finished. What's up that way?"

Mick stopped in the doorway and looked in the direction Abby pointed. The perpendicular shadows of the studs looked like a maze in the half-light to Abby, but Mick knew his way around. "The plans call for three bedrooms, two baths, and a little room—like an office or a nursery, I guess. So far I've only worked on this bathroom and bedroom. I don't need the rest of the space—except for tonight."

"I—"

"You can sleep up here," he said across her question, "and I'll stay downstairs, all right?"

"I can't put you out of your own bed!"

"The sofa opens up," he explained. "I used it all winter, in fact, to save heating this wing. Don't worry about me. If you get cold, there's an extra blanket under the bed."

"I'm the warm-blooded kind," Abby said, not thinking.

"Oh," Mick said, and he put his shoulder against the doorjamb. "That's interesting."

By some trick of light, Abby couldn't quite see his face, but she knew that Mick could see her expression perfectly. She tried to collect her poise, thinking that she had let her sophisticated facade slip just a little during their talk in the kitchen. She didn't want Mick to think she was as insecure as she was feeling. He was standing very close to her, though, and suddenly she couldn't make herself take a step away from him.

In fact, already she was feeling peculiar about sleeping in that big, unfinished part of the house. She felt as if she were on a Hollywood sound stage, and at any moment an evil phantom might come slinking out of the shadows. Abruptly, Abby thought that she didn't want to be alone up there. She wanted to stay close to Mick, to be protected by him.

But a Vanderbine couldn't be weak, she thought firmly. A Vanderbine would graciously accept Mick's hospitality and proceed to sleep like a baby, no matter how creepy the setting. Abby put on her act one more time. She inclined her head and said coolly, "What I meant was—"

"I know what you meant," Mick broke in, and there was a quiver of laughter in his voice. He folded his arms across his chest and said, "You were unintentionally provocative, so I forgive you. To be absolutely honest, Dear Abby, if I had any locks up here, I'd advise you to bolt your door tonight."

"But since there aren't any locks?" Abby asked, praying that her voice wasn't trembling. "Or even any walls?"

"I guess we'll have to rely on self-restraint."

"Yours?" Abby inquired before she could stop herself. "Or mine?"

Mick considered that answer, and the implications hung in the air like ripe apples ready to fall from a laden tree. Abby wanted to snatch back what she had said, but it was too late. She held her breath and wondered what he was thinking.

Then, slowly, Mick said, "I haven't figured you out yet, Dear Abby. One minute you're—" He stopped himself and then said, "There was only one time during the whole day that I was absolutely sure of what you were thinking."

"Oh? When was that?"

He stepped out of the shadow and took her wrist in his hand. "When I kissed you."

Though common sense gave a frenzied shout in the back of her mind, Abby didn't retreat. She could have ducked around the unfinished wall and escaped what was coming, but she didn't want to. She let Mick take her wrist in one hand, and then he pulled her against his own body. Around them, the silence was so absolute that Abby could hear her own heartbeat. It thumped within her so stridently that she was sure Mick could feel it against his own chest.

He curved one hand around the back of her head, letting his fingertips slip deliciously through her hair, and he tipped her face up to his. Abby had to force herself to look into his eyes. They were smoky-gray under his languid lashes, and he had a half-smile on his mouth. Softly, he said, "I wonder what you're thinking now."

He bent slowly, as if savoring every passing instant of denied pleasure. Abby watched his eyes, hoping wildly that her own were not so expressive. What was he seeing in her face? Desire? Dismay? Worse yet, uncertainty? In the split second before his lips touched hers, Abby let her lashes fall and instinctively lifted her face to meet his kiss. Mick's mouth was warm and sure, seeking to part her lips almost immediately. Her mind soared into a sweet darkness, swirling with sensations that were as misty as wind-whipped clouds.

His tongue was subtle, his breathing not quite so controlled. Against her cheek, Abby could feel his uneven sigh, against her lips she could feel his pulse, tripping almost as crazily as her own. She had unintentionally wedged one hand between her body and his chest, and now she moved it, sliding her palm higher until she met the hard contour of his shoulder. It was a signal of assent, perhaps, though an unconscious signal. Mick wound his arm around her body then and pulled her harder against his tall frame.

Abby melted into him, allowing her limbs to find their natural place against his. Their bodies sought each other by instinct and then fit perfectly together. Abby felt the warmth of his skin radiate through their clothing. She felt her breasts as they were squeezed erotically against his chest. She parted her lips more, allowing him to relish the silkiness of her mouth. He tasted of a thousand flavors that all melted into one exciting essence. Behind her head, his hand shifted, taking control of the kiss and its increasing power.

Blindly, Abby wanted to wrap both arms around his shoulders. She wanted to hold him, she realized, and comfort him. As he explored her mouth with growing fervor, Abby began to understand the message that Mick's stroking hands and insistent lips were unconsciously conveying. He's had a miserable day. His very life's work was in jeopardy, and he needed a release. He needed to vent his pent-up frustration. He needed to forget what had happened and concentrate on something totally sensual. He needed *her*.

He backed her into one of the unyielding wooden studs, pressing her spine into the upright board and shifting so that he could touch her differently. While he kissed her deeply, his left hand slipped swiftly up her ribs. He hesitated, then sought her breast with his palm. A rush of heat swept up from within herself so quickly that Abby gasped. Mick released her lips and found her throat with his mouth. She tipped back her head to breathe cooling air, but she felt her nipple harden beneath his touch. Already she was aroused, she thought. Already she was ready to surrender herself to him.

The thought that her body could respond to Mick so primitively brought Abby up short. She wasn't using her head. She was thinking with her body and with her emotions. A man couldn't suffer a business setback without needing comfort from the first woman to cross his path! She was acting foolishly.

Mick released her gradually, easing back from her now-trembling body. Abby heard him expel a long, unsteady sigh, and her eyes flew open once again. She stared up at him wondering how in the world she was going to talk him out of taking her to his bed and making love to her. For that matter, how was she going to talk herself out of the same thing? She could hardly stand up, and if Mick hadn't supported her body in his arms, she might have slipped to the floor.

"Well," Mick said in a voice that was close and husky, "I don't need a crystal ball, do I?"

"N-no," Abby said, holding his smoldering eyes with her own. "Neither do I."

"It could be very good, couldn't it?"

"Y-yes," Abby breathed, closing her eyes once again in an effort to regain her senses. Her head was swimming. "But..."

"But," Mick agreed, matching her whisper, "it might be even better if we waited."

Abby swallowed hard and tried to smile at him. "How good are you at postponing gratification?"

"Under normal circumstance, I'm very good. You?"

"I—I'm terrible, in fact. I've been known to tear the corners of my Christmas presents just to see what was inside."

"I can't believe that," he said just as lightly. "You don't seem the type."

Abby let her hand slip down Mick's strong shoulder until it came to rest on his forearm. She avoided his gaze and said, "I know it's my worst quality and someday I'll do something about it, but tonight—well, I can trust you to do the thinking for both of us, can't I?"

Mick took nearly a full minute to think that over, and during that time he moved to grasp her hand in his larger one. When he did speak finally, Abby could hear a curious smile in his voice. "That's a very nice rejection. Are you always such a lady?"

"No."

He smiled and leaned forward to press one kiss against her forehead. Softly, he said, "Good."

He let her go then, and Abby caught her balance. For safety's sake, she didn't look up at him and tried to sound cool, calm, and collected once again. She said, "Good night, Mr. Piper."

"Say my name."

Quietly, Abby said, "Good night—Mick."

That was enough, apparently. He turned and walked the length of the unfinished hallway. The darkness swallowed him, and soon his footsteps faded away, too. Abby stood for a long time as if rooted to the spot, wondering if he might come back. She wondered if she ought to *call* him back.

But she didn't and he didn't, and Abby undressed and slipped into the bed alone. She ought to be relieved, she told herself. She liked Mick. She wanted him to go on liking her, too. She didn't want to risk losing his attentions before he really gave them. And he had just come very close to discovering what kind of lady she really was—or wasn't.

She hadn't brought a nightgown at all, pink or otherwise. Did sophisticated ladies sleep in the nude?

CHAPTER SIX

MICK DIDN'T SLEEP. He couldn't. His brain kept going around and around with images of both Abby Vanderbine—alternately sweet and feminine or coolly unapproachable—and huge jars of tainted peanut butter—both sweet and deadly poisonous. He would have preferred thoughts inhabited by the lovely but puzzling Abby, but he realized wryly that erotic dreams might prompt him to charge upstairs and act like a long-denied sex maniac. He forced himself to think about peanut butter instead.

Except Mick found he couldn't organize his thoughts anymore as he tried to get comfortable on the couch. He was losing his marbles, all right. How in hell was a man supposed to think straight under the kind of circumstances in which he found himself? Simultaneously, his career was going down the drain and the most attractive woman to walk into his life in years was sleeping less than fifty feet away. Impossible. Mick jammed a pillow over his head and tried to sleep.

Morning came eventually, and he shot out of a convoluted dream as if he'd been catapulted by a cannon. He sat up on the couch abruptly.

Somebody was banging on the front door. Mick grabbed his jeans and his shoes and got into them quickly, his brain full of fuzz. What exactly had he been dreaming about? A woman? He yanked yesterday's shirt off the kitchen chair where he'd left it and pulled it on as he stumbled out the hallway and down the steps to the entranceway. When he opened the door, he knew he wasn't fully awake.

And those memorable words hit him in the face like a bucket of freezing water.

"We'd like you to answer a few questions, Mr. Piper."

The cops. Probably the FBI, too, judging by the size of the crowd. There was a whole mob of them out on his yard, and the driveway was full of cars, half with flashing lights on top. There was even a van from a television station out there, and some guys were scrambling out of it with cameras on their shoulders. All hell had broken loose.

"Mr. Piper, would you accompany me to the station, please?"

"Are you arresting me?"

"No, sir. We'd just like you to answer some questions."

"Why can't I answer them here?"

The officer did not blink. "We'd prefer that you come with us, Mr. Piper."

Mick suppressed a groan and turned around, putting his back to the throng of interlopers.

Then he saw a vision of a woman standing on the

steps above him. She was wearing one of *his* flannel shirts and nothing else. Her bare legs were long and wonderfully golden, and her blond hair was tangled into a froth of seafoam around her wide-eyed face. She was pale and beautiful in the morning and she clutched the shirt around her slender body like a woman who had been startled in her boudoir. When Mick's brain cleared, he recognized Abby Vanderbine.

"Hello," he said calmly to her, ignoring the voices of the police behind him.

"What's happening?" she asked, blinking those bewildered blue eyes in an effort to comprehend the madness.

"I'm being arrested. Except they're too polite to call it that," he said even as the cop grabbed his arm from behind. "Will you call Rob for me?"

"Yes, of course."

"Just tell him what's happened, but he's not to come for me," Mick commanded. "I don't want any of the family to get involved today—there will be bad publicity. Make him understand, Abby, please."

She nodded, still hugging her shirt against herself. "I will. What else?"

She was faster to wake up than he was, and Mick felt a rush of gratitude. He even managed a grin. "Make yourself some breakfast, all right?"

"Yes," Abby said, coming down the stairs to him on soundless bare feet. She touched his chest with one hand and looked up into his face.

She smelled marvelous, and her eyes were so expressive, so agonized, that Mick wanted to tell her everything was going to be okay. Except he wasn't sure of that himself.

"I'll come as soon as I can," she said.

He wanted to kiss her, but two policemen hustled him out the doorway before he could say another word.

The telephone call to Mick's cousin Rob was not easy. It was very difficult to find a way to tell someone that a member of his family had just been carted off to the jailhouse by a platoon of policemen. Rob had argued with her, too.

"I'm going down there right now," he roared, beside himself. "They can't do this to Mick!"

"But he especially said that he didn't want any of his family to get involved," Abby argued quickly. "I'm sure they're just going to question him and turn him loose. You can't help with that, Mr. Piper. I think we ought to respect Mick's thinking in this."

Rob had growled and muttered for several minutes, but Abby finally convinced him that it would do everyone more harm than good to surround Mick during this time. Rob hung up, ordering Abby to call him as soon as she knew something.

Then Abby took the time to shower and make herself a decent breakfast. She dressed in her suit again and pulled her hair into a sedate ponytail before taking her rental car into the town of Blue Creek. Mick had not asked *her* not to get involved. She intended to see for herself what kind of trouble he was in.

Abby found the police station with little trouble. She pushed her way through the gathered crowd of press and managed to talk to an officer who was manning the front desk. He waved in the direction of Mick's lawyer, a man named Calloway.

Clay Calloway was barely as tall as Abby, but he was barrel-chested and strong-looking, with a hound-dog kind of face—dark, sad eyes, and firm jowls. He was dressed in a rumpled suit, and his tie needed to be cleaned. Judging by those clues as well as his lack of a wedding ring and the way he watched one of the nearby woman reporters, Abby decided that Clay Calloway was a bachelor.

He was surprised when Abby sought him out in the crowd, and he looked delighted by her appearance until she introduced herself and her interest in Mick. He put two and two together, swallowed his obvious disappointment, and apparently decided she was safe to talk to.

"Mick was questioned already," he told her when he found them a quiet corner near a coffee-vending machine. "They're taking a break before round two."

"Will they let him go?"

"They'll have to charge him with a crime if they want to keep him," the lawyer said, slurping cold coffee from a Styrofoam cup. "Between you and me, they don't have enough evidence to hold him. I think this is a scare tactic, to get Mick to confess. Unfortunately, if he leaves before they're finished with their questions, he *looks* guilty."

"But he didn't do anything!"

Calloway grimaced. "That's the way the FBI works sometimes—especially in cases where there isn't *any* evidence and people are in danger. They rely on strategy. Mick hasn't been arrested. He's only being questioned."

"Certainly they had to have *some* clue that he was involved before they'd drag him here."

"I'm betting they figured out what substance was put into the peanut butter. They haven't told us yet, but whatever it was, it must be somehow traceable to Mick. We'll try to pin them down this afternoon."

"Can I see him?"

"Mick? No way." He threw his unfinished coffee into a trash can before turning back on Abby. "They've got him locked up tight in a cell—to 'protect' him, they say. But all they really want is to keep him from cryin' the blues to the press."

Abby closed her eyes, feeling miserable. Poor Mick. He had gone through this kind of thing before. No doubt sitting in a jail cell was going to remind him of the last time he suffered such indignity. At least this time he wasn't grieving his dead wife at the same time. Abby steeled herself against that image and looked up at Mr. Calloway. "You know," she said unevenly, "when they came to get him, he hadn't had any breakfast. Or dinner or lunch yesterday."

Calloway's face softened and he took the liberty of patting Abby on her shoulder. "Don't worry. Looking after my client includes making sure he gets fed. I'll take care of it."

Abby hesitated and then held out the package she had fashioned out of a paper bag. "I brought him a change of clothes."

"Oh, yeah? That was—uh, nice." Calloway accepted the package, but his gaze was sharp on Abby's face. "Listen, this may be out of line and I shouldn't be looking a gift horse in the mouth—but just who are you, anyway?"

Abby smiled ruefully. "I guess I'm the Lone Ranger."

He grinned. "I didn't recognize you without the mask."

Abby laughed. "I know this must look as if I'm an old and steady girl friend or something, but I only met Mick yesterday. I'm from Chicago. I came to do a story on his company, you see."

"You could have picked a better day to come."

"Right," Abby agreed with a sigh. "I feel like the bearer of bad luck."

"No, no," Calloway said cheerfully. "Anyone who

brings clean socks and worries that Mick doesn't get three square meals a day is anything but bad luck."

"Thanks," Abby said, and she decided that Mr. Calloway was a nice fellow indeed. If his legal skills were as good as his knack for understanding people, Mick had chosen a very good lawyer for himself.

Abby left the police station feeling useless. She was also disappointed that she had been turned away. She wondered how gruesome FBI questioning could become. Would they break out the rubber hose and force Mick to confess to something he didn't do? Just the thought of such a possibility made her shiver.

She drove to the Piper Peanut Butter offices and talked her way through the FBI's barrier. She intended to answer the telephone and see if there was any pressing business that she should convey to Mick. Using her old reporter's bravado, she argued that they couldn't deprive Mick Piper of his income, and if someone wasn't allowed to take care of business, the company might go bankrupt. It would be the FBI's fault, she declared. After a fifteen-minute discussion in which Abby expressed righteous indignation, they allowed her to pass through, first insisting that an officer watch everything she did.

Abby accepted, wanting to make sure that Piper Peanut Butter survived this crisis. If Mick was in jail, she could pitch in and help keep the company floating.

The office was a wreck. As soon as Abby opened the door, she realized that the law-enforcement officials had searched the premises. The filing cabinets hung open drunkenly, their contents strewn all over the floor. The desks had been rifled, and even the upholstery on Mick's office chair had been slit open for inspection. Abby was outraged that the place could have been left in such an appalling state. Furious, she set about clearing up.

The telephone rang several times, and Abby hastened to pick it up in hopes that there would be news of Mick's release. But it was only the press or other ghouls wanting information. Abby put most of them off. One call did interest her, however. It was a New York-based advertising agency that felt they could help.

"We can convince the public that it's safe to buy the peanut butter again," the executive told her. "Have Mr. Piper give us a call when things calm down."

Abby wrote down the number. In her opinion, it might be a good idea for Mick to discuss the possibilities with advertising experts.

Plenty of other calls came, and Abby answered them all as best she could. Some people wanted information, and others wanted to voice their opinions. Abby was polite but cool with all of them. A breathless medical student from a nearby university called to apologize for missing her appointment with Mick and wanted to reschedule. She had not seen or heard the news, because she was stunned when Abby told her that Mick would be unavailable until after the crisis had passed. The student promised to call back in a few weeks before she hung up.

There came no word from Clay Calloway as the day wore on. Abby straightened up the offices and did her best to put the filing system back together again, but Mick's lawyer didn't telephone. As evening approached, she decided to go back to Mick's house to wait for some word.

She stopped at the supermarket and bought a few supplies. Using Mick's keys, she let herself into the house. Jelly the cat greeted her like an old friend. She made a meal with enough for Mick, too, but when nine o'clock arrived and he still hadn't come home, she wrapped up the leftovers and put them into the refrigerator.

At ten o'clock, Clay Calloway called.

"Nothing," he reported. "We're not getting anywhere. If they don't charge Mick by morning, I'm going to scream bloody murder until they release him without any strings attached."

"But he's stuck in custody until tomorrow?"

"At least," Clay said grimly. "Shall I give him any messages?"

"From me?" Abby asked, startled. "Goodness, I can't—well, tell him that everything is okay at his office."

"You're looking after things? Great. Mick was afraid Rob was going to move in over there and do something crazy. Knowing you're standing guard will help Mick sleep a little better tonight, I'm sure. Listen, I've got to call Rob and Mick's dad. I'll see you tomorrow, okay?"

"Okay." Abby hesitated, then said impulsively, "Mr. Calloway—"

"Call me Clay."

"Clay," Abby said then, smiling, "would you tell Mick that—that I'm keeping my fingers crossed for him?"

"Is that all?" Clay asked, voice amused and loaded with implications.

"Yes," Abby said firmly.

"Okay," he returned. "Funny thing. He said something equally cryptic about you. I wasn't supposed to repeat it, though. Good night, Miss Vanderbine."

After he had hung up Abby sat for a long time in the kitchen of Mick Piper's house with Jelly on her lap and a cup of hot tea at her elbow. How odd, she thought, that she could feel so at home in a strange place.

CHAPTER SEVEN

ABBY SLOWLY WOKE in Mick Piper's bed the following morning to the sound of the bathroom shower running full blast. She sat up in bed, clutching the bedclothes to her near-naked body, straining to hear who had invaded the house. At that moment the shower taps were shut off, and the rattle of a towel rack reached Abby's ears.

Jelly, braver than Abby, leaped off the bed where he'd been sleeping and went to investigate.

The cat must have nudged open the bathroom door, because soon Abby heard Mick's voice sounding hushed, as if he didn't want to awaken anyone. "What are you doing here? I thought you were too busy cuddling up to notice me." A grudging pause came next in which Abby imagined that Mick may have touseled the ears of his pet, and then he said with more affection this time, "All right, shhh. You'll wake her up."

He sounded tired and on edge. She could hear it in

his voice. Abby thought that he must be thankful to be back in his own home after so many hours of high-pressure interrogation. She certainly couldn't expect him to be charming, however. *She'd* want to be alone after an infuriating experience like the one Mick had just endured. And chances were good that he might be downright unpleasant now that it was over. She couldn't blame him.

Abby figured she had less than two minutes to get dressed. She piled out of bed and snatched a red flannel shirt off the chair where she'd left it the night before. Any second he was going to come out of the bathroom and catch her undressed. Heaven only knew how much he'd already seen. Her jeans—the one item of clothing she never traveled without—were draped over the edge of the bed. She grabbed them hastily and pulled them on. Mick was about to see the sophisticated-lady image go down the drain, but it couldn't be helped. It would take her too many minutes to get buttoned into her skirt and blouse again. She zipped up her jeans and reached for her hairbrush.

But there wasn't enough time to make herself totally presentable. Mick came out of the bathroom. Since the bedroom didn't have any walls, Abby spun around and faced him through the studs, holding the hairbrush against her stomach.

"Oh," he said. "You're awake."

His grin was gone. Abby saw that at once.

No longer was there a light of youthful exuberance in Mick Piper's eyes. He was unshaven and looked haggard. And a little angry, too. There were puckers at the corners of his eyes, and the lines that ran from his nose to the corners of his usually curved mouth were deeper. The last two days had taken their toll. Mick no longer looked like a grown-up Huckleberry Finn.

Abby summoned her poise and edged cautiously to the doorway of the room. She smiled and tried to sound light. "And you're out of jail. Congratulations."

"Save it," he said, almost rude and definitely bitter. "They're probably going to come get me again before this thing is over."

"Oh." Abby blinked uncertainly. She hadn't expected him to be quite so disgusted. He was barely keeping his agitation in control, she could see. And he made quite a picture of the male animal standing before her in his bathrobe. The combination was unnerving. Awkwardly, she said, "That's—I'm sorry."

Mick had a towel in his hands and he was wearing a blue terry bathrobe that had been casually knotted around his waist. It was half open to show a wide expanse of his bare chest, his damp hair curling riotously there. He had buffed his head, but his dark hair was wet at the tips. He looked half-naked and dangerously casual about it.

Sauntering, Mick came to stand before her in the hallway. He seemed taller than Abby had remembered. But then, she realized, she was barefoot this time instead of teetering on her high-heeled shoes. Mick was not just big, but virile, too. Without his clothes, a lesser man might have looked silly, but Mick was completely male. Desirable . . . and threatening. Abby forced herself not to step back from him.

He made no bones about absorbing her appearance. In fact, he looked her up and down thoroughly and then raised one eyebrow in silent acknowledgment of the fact that she was wearing one of his shirts. Abby realized that she had unconsciously begun to hug the shirt against her body as if to hide herself from his raking inspection.

Then Mick reached. With his free hand, he touched Abby's chin, lifting her face so that he could see it better.

Abby held her breath. His fingers were warm, but she was unnerved by the lack of animation in his face. He didn't look into her eyes, but instead studied her face, her throat, her shoulders. Holding her chin, he simply drank in her appearance with something like hunger flickering in his gray eyes.

Abby wondered what he saw. She was afraid to speak.

Mick remembered himself finally. Like a man coming out of a dream, he shook his head to clear it and he seemed to be able to focus his attention again. He did not release her, but said mechanically, "I'm sorry about waking you up, but I couldn't wait to get into the shower. I had to get the smell of the Blue Creek jail out of my nose. If you want to go back to bed—"

"No, no," Abby whispered, hesitating to twist out of his grasp for fear he might reach for her again—in a different way. "I couldn't sleep anymore. How—how about some breakfast? Are you hungry?"

He released her reluctantly and touched his fingertips briefly to the loose ends of her blond hair. "Yeah, I guess so. Food and a shower were my reasons for roaring back here this morning. But now . . ."

He did not finish, but glanced down at the last buttons of the shirt that she had not taken the time to do up. He allowed his words to die away.

Automatically, Abby began to fasten the buttons. She interpreted his glance and unspoken suggestion immediately. Mick had come up for a shower and found her in his bed. Perhaps he had stood in the doorway and watched her sleep. What had he seen? What had he thought? Had he been tempted to forgo the shower and slide into the bed with her? Her stomach began to tingle at that possibility. How long had he watched her? What expression had been on his face? Had he decided to take a cold shower instead of a warm and soothing one?

Mick saw her expression and laughed shortly, snapping out of his trancelike state. "You don't have to look so mortified, Dear Abby. I have only lusted for you in my heart."

"I didn't—"

"So far at least," he added blandly. "Look, daydreaming about you at least made yesterday endurable. I had nothing to do but stare at four walls and answer the same three questions every half hour. Fantasizing kept me sane. I wish I had thought of you in a getup like that, though. You look terrific."

She hugged the shirt against herself all over again. In a rush, she said, "I didn't have any other clothes with me, and I thought it would be all right if I borrowed—"

"Forget it," he cut her off. "If I'd known you were making use of my clothes instead of that Fifth Avenue suit you had on before, I might have been almost content. Greta Garbo dressed like a lumberjack. Very nice."

"I'll return your shirt as soon as possible," Abby said stiffly, disconcerted by his manner. Before Mick had been fun and teasing about the sexual kind of attraction between them. Now, however, there was a different kind of tension in the air. Conscious that she might have sounded nervous, she explained unnecessarily, "I need to take my suit to the cleaner today. It's looking a little limp, you see."

"Limp?" he repeated, eyeing her anew. Slowly, he reached, and with great care he unfastened the top button of the shirt again. A cool rush of air touched Abby's throat, and she suppressed a shiver. Satisfied with the way she looked then, Mick said, "I can't imagine anything of yours being limp."

Abby colored and began, "I—it's—oh!" She ran her hand through her tangled hair in exasperation with herself, then smiled upward at Mick. "I'm acting like an idiot this morning! I—I must be groggy still. How about some breakfast to welcome you home?"

"Just breakfast?" Mick asked, not moving. "Is that a celebration?"

Abby laughed weakly and tossed her hairbrush onto the bed, determined to brazen her way out of a big problem before it got started. She folded her arms and joked, "Well, I could order some balloons and party hats—or maybe a giant cake for someone to jump out of, but you don't exactly look ready for a full-blown celebration yet. A little food will make you feel like your old self again, won't it?"

He smiled finally. Relenting, he stepped back to allow her into the hallway with him. "Maybe you're right."

"Then breakfast is coming right up."

He shoved Jelly gently out of his way with his foot and then followed her down the hallway. "I hope you made yourself at home during my absence."

"Completely," Abby replied, attempting to send him a cheery smile over her shoulder. "I've been shamefully at home, in fact. Thank you for letting me stay. I took care of Jelly and did some shopping for you."

"You didn't have to pay for your room with services like that," Mick said. "I was glad when Clay told me you were here. He said you were holding the fort at the office, too."

Abby laughed. "Attacking Indians use the telephone now. One of the calls was even obscene. Actually, it's the FBI who have the place thoroughly guarded."

"So I heard," Mick said grimly. "Have they ransacked the place looking for clues?"

Abby arrived in the kitchen and snapped on the lights. "Yes, they have." Mick wasn't the kind of man who needed to be shielded from the truth, she knew, and he wasn't in any kind of mood to joke around. She said, "They began in the office and tore everything to pieces. I tried to straighten things up, but you're going to have to go through the files yourself, I'm afraid. Then they moved into the plant, but I wasn't allowed inside to see what they were doing."

"No doubt they were trying to figure out how the drug got into the peanut butter."

Abby turned around to Mick in surprise. "Then it *was* a drug? They finally figured out what had contaminated the peanut butter?"

"Yep." Like a kid in the losing team's locker room after a game, Mick snapped the towel idly at one of the chairs by the table. He explained, "They knew what drug it was almost from the beginning, but they didn't want the press to know until they were sure."

"What was it?"

Mick glanced at Abby to read her expression. "Penicillin."

"Penicillin? That's not poisonous!"

"To people who are allergic to it, it is."

"Good grief! You mean—? Why would anyone put a drug like penicillin into food?"

"It's called industrial sabotage, my Dear Abby." Mick paced along the center island of the kitchen, sending Jelly scampering out of his way. "Either somebody has a real grudge against me or against my company or they're— well, just plain crazy."

Abby slid behind the counter with the cat, watching Mick as he spoke. He was prowling, restless and snapping the towel as he moved. Abby could see that he was holding a volatile combination of emotions at bay. Tentatively, she said, "Well, at least you're no longer a suspect."

"On the contrary," Mick said. "I seem to be number one on the FBI's hit parade at the moment."

Abby stared at him. "Why, for heaven's sake? Why would you do such a thing to your own company?"

"That's the only flaw in the FBI's theory. I don't have a motive. But the penicillin was a clue that led the police straight to me."

"Why?"

"Because," Mick said, stopping to look out the kitchen window at the backyard, "my wife died from the effects of a few tablets of penicillin."

"What?" Abby blurted out, too startled by that information to remember her manners.

"You heard me."

"I thought—you mean your wife's death was an accident?"

"No," Mick said, his head still averted so that Abby couldn't see his face. He stood very still. "It was suicide, all right. Laura was violently allergic to the stuff and knew it would kill her in a matter of minutes. I had been to the dentist a few days before and was taking penicillin because I'd had a wisdom tooth pulled. She took the pills that I was supposed to have—"

"Oh, dear," Abby said harshly, stopping him. How awful for Mick. She laid both hands flat on the counter and bent her head, eyes closed. As the facts fell into place in her mind, she felt sick. No wonder a man of Mick's qualities and attributes was living in such a small town and isolating himself from the rest of the world. He blamed himself for his wife's suicide, no doubt. She had used pills that were intended for him. And now some horrible person was using the same drug to ruin Mick's company.

Abby felt a hard lump start to congeal inside her throat, a lump of sympathy for a man who was struggling with more than just the future of his business. Without lifting her head, she said in an unsteady voice, "Let's not talk about—her, all right?"

Mick couldn't have missed her involuntary reaction, but he pretended he hadn't noticed. He shrugged and looked down at the towel in his hands, saying gruffly, "That was so long ago it hardly matters now. Except that whoever put the penicillin in the peanut butter may have known about Laura, you see. A typical criminal wouldn't think of using penicillin as a poison."

"You mean if he was serious about killing people, he should have used something different?"

"Sure. Arsenic's one possibility. Or even PCP, for crying out loud!" Mick controlled himself and swung away from the window, starting to pace again. "He could have bought something on any streetcorner! Penicillin only kills victims who are allergic to it. The FBI doesn't think that the average psychopath would have come up with the idea of using an antibiotic if he just wanted to hurt people at random."

"Penicillin was an odd method for suicide, and it's equally odd for industrial sabotage, is that it?"

"Right." Mick flicked the damp towel at the legs of the kitchen table he passed, and the blow made a loud *crack*. Jelly shot out of the room for safety's sake. Mick didn't notice. Abruptly, he demanded, "So why did this guy choose penicillin?"

"To point a finger at you?" Abby guessed hesitantly. "Or have I read too many murder mysteries?"

"I read murder mysteries, too. If Dick Francis were writing this, I'd guess that somebody made a halfhearted attempt at framing me."

"That's pretty far-fetched."

"Exactly," Mick retorted. "I don't want to believe that there is a real plot afoot to ruin Piper's. It's too bizarre. But why would some nut pick *my* peanut butter and decide to— Dammit, it's too crazy!"

"Well, thank God we found out before someone died."

Mick snapped the towel at the legs of a chair. *Bang!* The whole chair jumped at the force of the blow. Abby flinched. Mick was *angry* and she had missed the signs.

To cover her nervousness, she opened the refrigerator and began to unload it, putting a carton of eggs, a milk bottle, and some butter on the counter. Before he blew up completely, she had better feed him! Still trying to disarm him, she said, "It's so silly that the FBI would think that *you* would do such a thing."

Mick snorted. "Oh, they're still working on a case against me. Just because they turned me loose doesn't mean they've decided I'm innocent."

"That's ridiculous," Abby chided. She closed the refrigerator door and lifted a frying pan down from the rack over the stove. "I certainly hope they're also looking for the real criminal during all this."

"You bet your sweet—" He caught himself and said bitterly, "I'm sure they are. The FBI strikes me as a very efficient group."

"Let's hope so," Abby said gently, hoping she could

stay out of his way while he blew off steam. She hurriedly found a set of mixing bowls on a shelf and fumbled through them, clattering the crockery to mask her silence. French toast. Maybe that would charm him into an even-tempered mood.

She had a pretty good idea how hard it had been for Mick to hang onto his composure. He had been treated unfairly and imprisoned unjustly. Now he was on the brink of exploding. He was pacing, growling, snapping, barely keeping his anger in check. She was going to have her hands full if she didn't get him seated at the table soon and calmly eating his breakfast. She broke three eggs into the bowl.

Suddenly, Mick threw the towel into one of the kitchen chairs and jammed his hands into the pockets of his bathrobe. "The worst part is my family! My company is dying, but I can fight that. Even my own reputation— which, thanks to the press, is now that of a nut case—"

"The press will certainly report that you've been released without any charges brought against you."

"Not before the damage is done to my family! Dammit!" Mick exploded. *"They're* the ones who are suffering needlessly! Every Piper from here to Chicago is going to be affected by this mess!"

"They understand, I'm sure," Abby said, glad she had the kitchen island between herself and Mick. She clung to it and forced her voice to sound soothing. "Your cousin is very concerned, and he says that the rest of your family genuinely wants to help."

"Of course they do!" Mick shouted, glaring at her. "That's the way they *are,* for godsake! But damn, I hate to be the one whom they've always got to rally around. Why should their products suffer because I'm in a jam again?" He kicked one of the chairs out of his way and sent it skidding. "You know what the worse feeling in the world is? Being helpless. I hate this!"

"Sit down," Abby directed, doing the best imitation of her mother that was possible. Quiet but unyielding, that was it. Abby hadn't realized how much courage it took to be quiet and gracious during someone else's temper tantrum. She was trembling inside, but she forced herself to sound calm. "Please, Mick. You're only making it worse on yourself. I'll make your breakfast, and then maybe you'll feel better. Why don't you sit down?"

"I don't feel like sitting." Mick faced Abby across the island, his fact taut, his eyes flinty. He looked at her and said bluntly, "I don't feel like eating, either."

"You obviously need some way of burning off your excess energy," she argued gently. "Maybe you should— say, why don't you go play basketball? That's it! Go slam things around outside before you break something in here."

For a moment, Mick just looked angry. He glowered at Abby as if she were the root of all his problems.

Then, abruptly, he let his gaze slip down to the shirt she was wearing. It was loose around her slender figure, but it didn't conceal the smooth curve of her breasts and the neat tuck of her waist. And Abby knew that her jeans were so worn that they clung to her hips and thighs and skimmed her slim legs in a subtle and perhaps alluring way. From the way he looked at her, though, she felt as if she was wearing the sheerest nightgown created by Fredricks of Hollywood.

"Go play basketball," she repeated, suddenly feeling very nervous indeed. "It will be therapeutic."

He said, "I can think of a lot of things that would be therapeutic, Dear Abby."

She met his gaze and said, "No, Mick."

The moment snapped, and Mick controlled himself. His face looked numb, his eyes were expressionless, as though the effort to suppress whatever was inside him took all his energy. He said simply, "Basketball. Good idea."

And he left the kitchen abruptly.

Abby put her hands on the counter again to steady herself. Close call. Mick Piper was burning up inside, she knew. He was angry and frustrated and full of guilt and, yes, some humiliation, too. He didn't like the corner into which circumstances had pushed him. And in the short time Abby had begun to know Mick, she understood that he wasn't the kind of man to shrug off any of the troubles that were growing around him. He took everything personally.

Abby understood her position, too. She was the only person in Mick's world right now in whom he could confide. He felt loyalty for his family—so he couldn't turn to them and drag them into the public eye in the process. But he could turn to Abby and vent his emotions without risking consequences. She was convenient. He needed someone, and she was there.

He had wanted more than soothing talk from Abby. He had wanted much more, in fact.

Yes, it had been a very close call.

CHAPTER EIGHT

MICK REAPPEARED in a pair of abbreviated athletic shorts. He put a tape on the stereo and went outside to play shadow basketball. Along with the music, Abby soon heard the synchronized thump-thump-thump-*crash* of dribbling and shooting.

She decided that Mick's mood was always reflected by the music he chose. He had an enormous sound system set into the pantry closet, and he had arranged huge stereo speakers all over the house. Apparently, he liked listening to rock and roll whereever he was, and the expensive equipment was his one true extravagance. While he shot baskets, the whole house reverberated with the pounding, driving, sometimes bloodcurdling sounds of the Rolling Stones.

Abby left Mick alone. His choice of music clearly indicated that he needed to work off some aggressions.

So she listened to the Stones and puttered around the house, first making the bed, then getting herself cleaned up into a halfway presentable state, and then she decided to use the eggs she had broken to make a soufflé. She felt almost housewifely as she bustled about the kitchen.

The whole morning, however, was interrupted by the ringing of the telephone and the doorbell. Abby appointed herself to the task of intercepting Mick's phone calls, since he showed no interest in talking with anyone. For the most part, it was the press who called and asked to speak to him. Abby acted as a buffer. She shielded Mick from the high-pressure nonsense of unwelcome publicity. It seemed that everyone wanted a new angle on the poisoned peanut-butter story. She hung up on an obnoxious man who claimed to be a reporter for a particularly sensationalist tabloid. At the front door, she turned away a persistent young woman who carried an unlikely looking press pass from *The New York Daily News* and who had a sly smile on her face when she said she wanted Mick's life story—every gory detail of it.

Before lunchtime, the doorbell chimed again, and Abby prudently checked through the window before she opened the door. It was only Rob Piper, though, looking florid and harried but dressed in another spiffy three-piece business suit.

He brushed past Abby, saying over the roar of the Stones, "Where's Mick?"

"Good morning," she replied coolly. Even if Rob *was* making a big show about helping Mick through this crisis, Abby wasn't overwhelmed by the man's charm. She followed him up the stairs into the house and said, "He's outside playing basketball."

"Good," Rob said. "I'm glad he's staying out of sight

of the press. I'll go out and speak to him. Is there any coffee, Angie?"

"Abby. I'll make some."

"Good. And turn down that music, will you? I can't hear myself think."

Rob let himself out through the patio doors, and soon the thudding sound of Mick's basketball ceased. Abby could hear the cousins' voices as they talked. She made a pot of coffee, took another phone call from some crazy lady in St. Louis, and then carried a tray with cups, the steaming pot of coffee, and a jug of hot water for her tea out to the patio. She took along a towel for Mick, and purposely did not turn down the volume of the music.

Rob was sitting at the glass-topped umbrella table, drumming his fingers and speaking very fast.

Mick, his whole body gleaming with perspiration in the dazzle of morning light, stood just a few yards away, listening. He toyed with the basketball, occasionally bouncing it on the concrete to punctuate the lecture that his cousin delivered. Wearing nothing but his short shorts, white shoes, and a soaked sweatband around his hair, Mick looked magnificent. His body was a shining pillar of muscle and bone. He did not look the least bit tired from his exertions.

". . . so no matter what Dad says," Rob concluded, "I think it's obvious that you should lie low for a few days. Don't encourage any more publicity, and for godsake don't go around playing Sherlock Holmes! Let the police do the work and keep out of the limelight."

Abby set the tray down beside Rob's elbow and glanced up at Mick. He had been listening to his cousin, but he was watching Abby. He attempted a smile for her, but it looked grim.

"Coffee," Abby announced, interrupting the discussion. "And a snack. Mick, sit down and eat."

Surprisingly, he obeyed her. His stride was slow, but fluid and easy. He took the bright yellow towel from Abby and even allowed her to pry the basketball from his possession. She pulled out a chair for him and put aside the basketball, then poured him a cup of coffee and arranged a fluffy piece of her soufflé on a small plate. Then, after silently tucking a napkin into Mick's hand, she turned to play hostess for Rob.

"The whole family is distressed by what's going on," Rob said, ignoring Abby as though she were a new housemaid. "Nobody wants to see you get any deeper into trouble, Mick," he added.

"I haven't talked to any reporters," Mick said, using the towel on his still unshaved face, then putting it around his neck. "Abby's been putting them off since this whole thing got started."

"Good," Rob said, glancing briefly at Abby as she passed him a cup. "Keep it up," he said to her. "Keep him here, and in a few days we'll decide how to get things back to normal. If that's possible."

Abby said, "Of course it's possible."

Rob glowered at her as she sat down beside Mick and began to make herself a cup of tea. "I'm not so sure. But perhaps it's too early to make those kinds of judgments. The first order of business is to make sure Mick isn't connected with this unfortunate affair."

"He isn't," Abby said flatly.

"We don't think so," Rob agreed. "But not everyone else is so sure. What did the FBI have to say?"

"Nothing. They asked *me* questions, not the other way around."

"What exactly did they ask?"

Mick shrugged. "Who, where, why. Did I have any access to drugs? Was there anyone blackmailing me into doing something crazy, that kind of thing. All shots in the dark."

"So they don't have any idea who might have done it?"

"Other than me? No."

"You're still the best suspect, then."

"Yep. I must look very guilty to them."

Rob hesitated, as if unhappy about the subject he was about to introduce. He must have decided to jump directly to the point, for he sighed and said, "Mick, tell me about the Telluride Insurance Company."

Mick swallowed some coffee and looked surprised. "Telluride? What have they got to do with anything?"

"It's the insurance company you do business with, right?"

"Sure. For years."

"And you're well covered?"

"I think so. A buddy of mine from college started the company. I was one of the first clients he— Say, what's this about, Rob?"

Rob began to eat his portion of the soufflé so quickly that he could hardly have been tasting it. Around his mouthful, he said, "The FBI started checking. You've got extraordinarily good coverage, Mick."

"What do you mean by extraordinarily good?"

"Unusually good, let's say. Did you know that you are protected for lawsuits brought against your company? That means that if all those people who have been affected by the penicillin decide to sue you, your insurance company will pick up the tab. That's *very* unusual insurance coverage."

"I see," Mick said heavily.

"I don't," Abby said. "What's wrong with that?"

"It looks suspicious," Mick told her, meeting her eyes fleetingly before looking away.

"Very suspicious," Rob noted. "Companies rarely protect themselves against lawsuits unless they expect to *have* lawsuits brought against them. Like manufacturers of dangerous chemicals, maybe. But a peanut-butter maker? Why do you have insurance like that, Mick?"

"It's no big deal," said Mick, pushing aside his plate without touching the soufflé. "My friend opened an insurance office a few years ago. He needed clients to get started. My company was doing okay, and I could afford to help him out, that's all."

"You know how this looks to the FBI, though."

Mick sighed shortly. "Look, there are lots of ways to make me look guilty, Rob. But the bottom line is that there's no motive for me to ruin my own company. I *didn't do it.*"

"I know, I know, but the FBI—"

"The FBI can go to hell," Mick snapped.

"They're going to send you someplace just as unpleasant if they keep finding tidbits of evidence against you!"

"Look, dammit—"

Abby touched his arm to silence him. What she wanted to do, however, was throw a saucer at Rob Piper to shut him up! Couldn't he see that Mick didn't need to be told all this? Holding Mick's arm, she could feel him shudder with the effort it took to control himself. He was feeling rotten enough without lectures from his panicky cousin! She let go of his arm and pulled the small plate back to the spot in front of Mick. She said, "It's silly to argue. We're all on the same side, and you don't need to get

more upset than you are already. Whatever evidence the
FBI digs up about Mick can be disproved bit by bit, and
we know that. We shouldn't go haywire in the meantime."

"I am certainly not—"

"Of course not," Abby said hastily. "But we shouldn't
be frightened by what might appear to be growing evidence against Mick. We know it's all trumped up. It
won't be hard to prove he's innocent when the time
comes. Just take one step at a time for now, all right?
Rob, you look hungry. Would you like another piece?"

"Yeah." He shoved the plate across the table to her,
looking sullen. Into the resulting silence, he said abruptly,
"Look, I'm sorry, Mick. You know I don't mean to point
my finger at you. I'm just trying to make sure you don't
get framed for this, that's all."

"I won't get framed."

"Well, the insurance thing looks bad, and we've got
to find a way of explaining it to the cops. I'll call your
buddy at Telluride, okay? We'll get him to back up your
story."

"All right," Mick said, sounding deceptively resigned.
One look at his face told Abby that he was far from
feeling peaceful, though. He toyed with the cup before
him, staring into the coffee without seeing it. His jaw
was clenched.

"And if anything else turns up, I'll take care of it.
Between me and Angie here, we'll take care of you,
Micky."

A muscle quivered in Mick's jaw. But quietly he said,
"Thank you."

Rob pulled the second helping of soufflé toward himself and apparently dismissed the subject. "This is great

stuff, honey. You make it yourself?"

"Yes."

"Great stuff," Rob repeated, shoveling a mouthful. "Give me your recipe, and I'll pass it along to my wife."

Abby wasn't listening. She could hardly tear her gaze from Mick. He looked awful, his face tense and white. She ached to touch him again, wanting to comfort him. The last thing he needed was somebody else coming to his rescue, though. He would shake her off, she was sure. He hated being taken care of—that was clear from the way he reacted to Rob's solicitousness. Abby made an effort to pay attention to Rob instead and said, "The recipe came out of a cookbook. It's nothing special."

Chewing, Rob nodded. "It's good, though. What're you drinking there?" He pointed at her cup.

"Tea." Abby tried to smile. "I've never been a coffee drinker. This was the last teabag, though. I guess I'll have to switch over, won't I?"

Rob grunted. "Yeah. Listen, since you're here takin' care of things with the telephone and all, can I run some errands for you? Mick? You need anything from town?"

"No."

"The cupboards are a little bare," Abby said tentatively. "If Mick is supposed to stay here and out of sight, he could use a few supplies from the supermarket."

Rob nodded. "Okay, make a list. I'll send Miriam to the store and bring the stuff out this afternoon. Plan on enough stuff to take care of him for at least five days, huh?"

"Five days?" Mick demanded, appalled. "For crying out loud, Rob!"

"It's for your own good," Rob said, and then he looked sorrowful. "And for the rest of the family, of course. Did

I tell you that Dad's sales have fallen off already?"

"Yes," said Mick shortly. He hunched forward and put both elbows on the table, his head down, palms massaging his temples. "You told me."

"And Sis's customers are starting to make noises about cutting back on their deliveries, too." Rob sighed. "This hasn't just been hard on you, y'know. The whole family is feeling the pressure."

"I know, I know."

"Not that we don't want to help, of course. We're one hundred percent behind you." Rob sat forward so that his head was just a few inches from his cousin's. He dropped his voice and said, "We all care, Micky. We love you. Remember how Sis used to tag along after you in high school? She'd still like to be doing it! And just last night I was thinking of the way you took care of me on the football squad when I was havin' so much trouble with the coach."

Mick did not answer.

"And when you and Laura—well, you know how I felt about her, Mick. Even when she chose you over me I wasn't angry, because—well, you're like a brother to me. Havin' Laura in the family—" His voice caught. "Well, you and she—"

That was too much. Abby couldn't stand to hear another word. She stood up abruptly. "I'll go make up that list," she said, choking on her words. She bolted for the doorway and left the men alone to talk. A minute longer, and she was going to cry.

She ran into the kitchen and stood for a full minute, hugging her face with her hands and holding back her tears. She had never felt so sorry for anyone in her life, and she hated Rob Piper for how miserable he was making Mick. Bringing up Laura at a time like this! Why did Mick let his cousin go on that way?

Because Mick obviously loved his family as much as they did him. He wouldn't shout at Rob and tell him to mind his own business. He would listen and obey and suppress his anger and frustration. To protect his family, Mick was going to have to do the hardest thing of all. Nothing.

Rob came into the kitchen two minutes later, a big white handkerchief in his hand that he was using to wipe his face. When he spoke, his voice was still gruff with emotion. "Do you have that list yet?"

"Yes, yes," Abby said, scribbling as fast as she could. "Just a few staples, that's all. I think Mick must be accustomed to eating out."

"He has dinner with each of us every week," Rob explained, and he stuffed his handkerchief back into his pocket. "It's very kind of you to be looking after my cousin, Miss Vanderbilt. We appreciate your attentiveness when we can't do it ourselves. My stepmother would be out here like a shot if we weren't afraid of the publicity repercussions."

"It's no trouble," Abby said awkwardly. "I'm glad to be able to help in a situation like this. Here. Juice and bread—things like that."

Rob pocketed the list and spent a brief moment studying her. "You look like a smart young woman, I think. I hope you have no illusions about what's going on here."

"Illusions?" Abby blinked in confusion. "About what?"

"My cousin is in a precarious emotional state," Rob said bluntly. "I hope you can help him through it without adding to his concerns."

Abby nodded. "Yes, I see what you mean. I—I'll try, Mr. Piper."

"Call me Rob," he said, "since it looks like you're getting close to the family." Then he turned to go. "Keep him here, all right? I'll come back this afternoon."

Abby let him find his own way out of the house, and she waited in the kitchen until she knew she had collected her composure. They were starting to depend on her now. Calm again, she went out onto the patio.

As the Rolling Stones played, Mick was still sitting at the table, looking unhappy. That unhappiness seemed so unnatural on him that Abby's heart contracted once again. She determined to be cheerful, though. Mick didn't need any more gut-wrenching scenes.

Sliding into the chair beside him, she said over the music, "What's the matter, Mr. Peanut Butter? Don't you eat soufflés?"

Mick tried to rouse himself out of his reverie, but could only manage a wooden smile. "I'm not very hungry."

"I don't believe it. A man your size ought to be wolfing down everything in sight by now. When was the last time you had a real meal?"

He grinned a little. "What day is this?"

Abby winced. "You are a sad case, all right. Here. I'll spoon-feed you, if that's what it takes. Try it."

Like a good boy, Mick took the bite of soufflé that she offered, but he made no pretenses about savoring the flavor. When he had swallowed, he said, "I should be thanking you, too, for looking after me, you know."

"No," she said firmly, gathering another mouthful onto the fork. "You've done enough thanking for one day. I don't need it. Your cousin, though—"

"I shouldn't listen to him half the time, should I?" Mick asked. "I should learn to turn off my hearing aid when he gets started with his martyr routine."

"Is he a martyr?" Abby asked when she had fed him another bite of food.

Mick nodded. "Always. He knows all the right buttons to push to make me feel awful, and he's been doing it since we were kids. It works every time."

"Today it was rotten of him!"

He smiled at her vehemence. "You're certainly springing to my defense, aren't you? The tigress protecting her—what am I, anyway?"

"Not a cub, that's for sure. I *am* acting like an overprotective mother, aren't I? Making you eat and cooing over your health."

Mick took the fork from her hand, looking amused finally. "This is good. I'll eat it myself now, I promise, and you can stop cooing. I already have a mother, you know."

Abby relinquished the fork and sat back with a rueful smile on her face. "Okay, I won't mother you anymore. What would you like, instead?"

Mick met her gaze and didn't answer. Then he concentrated on his plate and began to eat without responding to her question. It hung in the air as the last chords of a thrumming guitar faded into silence. What Mick wanted did not need to be said aloud.

Abby felt light-headed suddenly. In the space of a few seconds, she was nervous all over again. She cleared her throat and whispered, "I see."

Mick glanced at her, and there was a gleam of light in his eyes when he saw how the change of subjects affected her. "What do you see?"

"That you—that I—"

"Yes?"

"That I'm playing with fire when I—before we really know each other very well."

"I think we know each other well enough."

"For..." Abby was suddenly afraid to say it. She avoided his gaze and couldn't continue.

Mick said gently, "I'm not asking for anything more, Dear Abby. Honest. Just having you here is very nice."

Abby released a tense sigh and managed to smile shyly at him. "Thank you."

"But," Mick continued with care, "I can't necessarily promise that I will continue to respect what kind of lady you are. You're very nice, very gracious, very gentle. Abby, that's a combination that makes a man want to behave in a way that's anything *but* gracious and gentle."

"Mick, if you'd like me to go—"

"I don't want you to go," he said just as softly. "I want you to stay, of course. But I want you to understand if you *do* stay here that I'm not exactly at my best these days. I can't promise I'm going to act like the mature and sophisticated guy I really am. We could end up throwing furniture at each other. Or making love like a couple of frantic newlyweds. Thank heaven you're too classy to get carried away in either direction."

Abby didn't smile. She didn't contradict him, either. She wanted to touch him again, but she knew it would be a mistake. She wanted to hold Mick's hand and smooth his hair and kiss his cheek. She looked at his solemn gray eyes and the straight mouth that had curved so easily into a happy-go-lucky smile before. Now he needed someone who understood him, who would listen to him and not use emotional blackmail to force him to stay shut up like a prisoner in his own home. Perhaps he also needed the control he thought she could provide. He needed a cool, sophisticated lady to help hold him together. He needed her.

Another man had needed help once, too. Abby thought

of the appliance-store owner who had fallen into despair after his business failed. She couldn't bear the thought that the same kind of thing might happen to big, vital, happy Mick Piper. Would they throw furniture? Or make love?

"I'd like to stay," she said finally.

"I'm glad," he said, and he touched her cheek.

He traced a line on her delicate skin with his fingertip, pausing only when he reached the corner of her lower lip. There, he hesitated.

Abby held very still and waited, her eyes wide.

Slowly, like a man afraid he was about to frighten a skittish waif, Mick sat forward in his chair. He drew his fingertips down to her throat and, probing gently, he found her pulse. It was fluttering, Abby knew. She couldn't seem to inhale a breath, either. Mick had discovered the fragility of her composure.

Softly, he said, "Abby, Dear Abby. You're lovely."

Perhaps the music had begun to blast again, but Abby was aware only of the sound of rushing wind inside her own head. She closed her eyes at the last instant, and the butterfly-soft caress of Mick's lips on hers felt like the merest ray of warm sunshine. He smelled wonderfully of the spring sun and exercise—superbly male. Inside, Abby felt her body begin to respond instinctively to his proximity. She couldn't stop herself. She began to tingle inside—with longing.

But Mick ended the kiss as gently as he had started it. He eased back in his chair, and before she could smother the sound, she released an unsteady sigh. It was almost a moan.

Mick said her name again, barely audibly this time. He tipped her chin higher and then impulsively returned to kiss her again—swiftly, harder. He found her mouth and immediately savored its shape with his tongue. Abby parted her lips at once, and her mind began to cloud with unexpected sensual images. She wanted to touch him suddenly, to slide her palms up the muscular contours of his chest and feel his heartbeat beneath her hands. She wanted to trace the muscle in his shoulders and then wrap her arms around his neck. But Mick restrained her before her impulses became reality. He captured one of her hands in his and held her so hard that it almost hurt.

A different kind of man might turn her loose and take her in his arms, but Mick did not. He respected the kind of woman he thought she was. He held her fast instead, unconsciously allowing her passions to seethe.

Through her parted lips, Mick languidly swiped her tongue with his own. He pressed deeper into her trembling mouth, demanding some response from her. Abby thought fleetingly of pulling away, but she could not make herself do it. She wanted more. She tilted her mouth, making the contact more perfect, more sensual. She allowed her tongue to explore his, savoring the elusive flavor that was Mick's alone. He was gentle, yet insistent; warm, yet capable of evoking a greater heat in her. He was forceful, yet inquiring. Abby's mind suddenly went blank, and for a long moment the universe narrowed to include only the two of them.

And then it was over. The kiss lessened and became little more than the feathery touch of flesh on warmer flesh. When they were finally a centimeter apart, Abby opened her eyes and blinked, unsure of what had happened. She felt changed inside, as if one kiss had altered her whole view of herself and this man whom she barely knew. No, they wouldn't throw furniture at each other.

Mick remained close to her, for Abby had somehow twisted in his grasp and was holding his hand as tightly as he held hers. He smiled, and his dark eyelashes did not quite veil the sparkle in his eyes. In a voice that had gone surprisingly husky, he said, "Dear Abby, I think you'd better let me go play some more basketball before I think of a way to muss you up a little."

CHAPTER NINE

MICK TRIED HIS DAMNEDEST to keep his hands off her.

He preferred shooting baskets to watching Abby Vanderbine putter around his kitchen. It unnerved him to see her handling his possessions, making his coffee, answering his telephone. And it wasn't that she had moved in like a pushy girl friend, Mick realized. The problem was that he *felt* as if she'd been a part of his home for a long time. She fit in. It was disconcerting to have a woman slip into his life so effortlessly.

There hadn't been many women since Laura, either. There hadn't been *any* with whom Mick felt the urge to spend more than a few hours at a time. Abby was different. He enjoyed her presence and didn't feel pressured to talk all the time when she was around. She was gentle and quick and classy.

But her casual, big-city sophistication wasn't what attracted Mick most. Her straight back, her lifted chin, her direct gaze were all very arresting. But now and then, Abby allowed a little of her vulnerability to show, and that sweetness affected him more strongly than if she had thrown herself into his arms. He saw her laugh with too much delight or hesitate uncertainly once in a while, and those clues let him know that she wasn't quite so poised as she hoped she was. It was charmingly feminine.

Mick wished he could honestly say that he liked having Abby around because she was pleasant and gentle and all the things a loyal friend should be during a crisis. But that wasn't all.

He wanted her. She was irresistible—a woman that any man would have a hard time keeping his hands off of. Mick's mouth went dry when she bent close to take his cup away. His brain turned to mush every time she picked up the telephone and tipped her head to pin the receiver between her shoulder and ear, exposing that long, milky throat of hers to the light. He was glad she had pulled the blond silk of her hair back into a stark ponytail, because all morning he had itched to weave his fingers through it, drag her face up to his, and kiss the stuffing out of her. And why did she have to wear that shirt of his, for crying out loud? It was far too big and concealed more than was fair! His imagination was going on overload.

But to attack Abby Vanderbine like a hillbilly's sex-starved coon hound would be a terrible mistake, Mick knew. He would only embarrass himself and repel her.

So he stayed out of her way and kept a safe distance. She wisely allowed him his privacy, but he suspected that she was doing it because she thought he was worried about his company. He was, of course, but some distractions were just too difficult to ignore. Mick didn't want to shock Abby by grabbing her up in his arms and carrying her up to his bedroom. He hoped that shooting baskets would keep his mind off his assorted troubles.

He could still think, at least. While he played, he ran over the possibilities again and again. Who could have put penicillin into his peanut butter?

After a while, he showered once more and got on the telephone to make some inquiries on his own. He called the plant foreman and cross-examined him for the better part of an hour. He called Clay Calloway and checked on the FBI's progress. Zilch. But at least the telephoning gave Mick the feeling that he was still capable of doing *something* useful. He sat for a long time on the patio, staring at the horizon and thinking through every step of peanut-butter production and trying to decide who had the best opportunity to slip penicillin into the jars. Unfortunately, there were a great many possibilities. And Mick couldn't think of a rational motive for any of them.

Rob returned at about five o'clock, laden with groceries from the supermarket. He didn't stay long, thank heaven. Mick didn't want to hear any more sermons from his cousin.

Mick helped Abby unpack the provisions and hung around the kitchen making idle conversation with her while she fixed a salad and prepared some steaks for the grill. He cooked those himself, and they ate together on the patio and discussed restaurants, for some reason he couldn't remember later. Perhaps Abby was just trying to get him to think about something other than peanut butter for a while. When he had finished his meal, his first in several days, Mick decided he was very glad to have her company. He'd be going crazy without her.

They went inside together and put their dishes in the sink.

"We can wash them later," Abby said. "I'll make you

some coffee and we can sit outside until the sun sets. It's warm enough, don't you think?"

Mick agreed, and while Abby measured the coffee, he found himself pacing again. He walked up and down the length of the kitchen island, unconsciously drumming his knuckles on the counter. He had to keep moving, and he grimly decided that the peanut-butter dilemma was only half the reason for his agitation. He also paced to keep his distance from Abby. In the half-light, she looked incredibly delicious, amazingly ladylike. Yes, he'd better keep himself under control.

She put the kettle on the stove for herself, saying, "Your cousin brought me some more tea from the store. Wasn't that nice of him? I had forgotten to put it on my list, but he must have remembered that I mentioned it."

Skeptical, Mick said, "My cousin rarely does something nice unless it's for a reason. He's probably decided we can't get along without you, so he's resorting to bribery."

Abby made a cheerful face at him as she opened the new box of teabags. "I thought I'd coaxed you out of your grouchy spell. I think Rob was just being nice— making up for calling me by the wrong name since we met."

"That was probably on purpose, too. Rob is always thinking, Dear Abby. You'll find that out."

She worked up her courage and said, "I'd like to find out a lot of things."

The telephone rang suddenly, however, preventing him from asking for a clarification. After the second ring, Abby turned to Mick and tipped her head in that way that made his heart flop like a landed fish. "Do you mind me playing your secretary?" she asked. "Or would you rather answer that yourself?"

"Do you think it's safe for me yet?"

She shook her head, smiling, and headed briskly for the phone again. "Frankly, no. I never realized how many peculiar people there are in the world. This afternoon somebody called who claimed to be your Aunt Margie from Tucson, but she made the mistake of starting to tell me how she used to sleep with you when you were a boy, and she got rather graphic before I realized she couldn't possibly be your real aunt." She calmly dusted off her hands on the towel that hung on the refrigerator door before reaching for the receiver. "I think your first order of business tomorrow is to get your number changed. Hello?"

Mick grinned unconsciously at the image of Abby intercepting obscene phone calls. He moved across the rug and into the den area. A fire might be nice later, he thought and bent on one knee at the hearth to heft some logs into place. As he worked, he listened to Abby's voice behind him. It was odd that one woman could have so many tones, he thought. When she talked with him, her voice had a wonderfully warm timbre. On the telephone, though, she sounded tough and businesslike. He reached for the long matches, lulled by the serenity of being protected by a capable lady.

"Michael?" she asked sharply. "May I ask who's calling please? His mother? No, I'm afraid—oh." She paused and glanced across the island toward Mick. Her eyes looked uncertain as they sought his. Suddenly, she blushed, startled, and directed her attention to the phone. "No, I haven't seen— Yes, yes, of course." Abby turned bright pink and practically threw the receiver at him.

No one in the world called him Michael except his own mother, so Mick was already halfway across the kitchen, dusting his hands on the seat of his jeans as he came. He took the phone from a flustered Abby and said, "Hi, Mom."

"Darling," came the familiar, brassy voice, "who *is* that woman? She wasn't going to let me speak with my own son!"

Watching Abby beat a hasty retreat, Mick grinned and said, "She's a friend, Mom."

"What kind of friend? I had to tell her about the birthmark on your *tush* to get her to—"

Mick laughed, feeling a rush of pleasure inside. "No wonder she blushed. She's guarding me from the savage press, that's all. How are you?"

"Darling, what do you *expect?*" she cried in tones Mick knew so well. "My firstborn child is *splattered* over the most disgusting newspapers in the country for some ridiculous reason, my adopted son is tearing around the countryside like a *madman,* and your sister has locked herself in her bakery and spends her time crying over *bread* dough." Beth Piper didn't pause for a breath. "Your father, on the other hand, is so furious that he won't speak to *anyone,* including me. But he keeps muttering about calling his friend on the Supreme Court. I haven't the heart to tell him that the man died five years ago."

"At least you're rising to the occasion."

"I'm worried," she retorted, "that's what I am. And *frustrated*. Robbie says we all have to sit on our hands until the publicity dies down, and you know how that makes *me* feel!"

Mick withheld a sigh. "It's mutual, Mother."

"I'm sure," she said, slowing down and sounding truly sympathetic finally. After a pause, she said in a gentler voice, "Michael, I feel sick about what's happening. Is there anything I can do? Really?"

Mick leaned against the wall and closed his eyes,

rubbing his forehead with one hand. It was easier listening to his mother rant than to have her talking like this. "I don't think so. Rob's probably right. We just keep to ourselves for a few days until things cool down. If the FBI doesn't have a handle on this mess by then, though, you can bet the Piper clan is going to clear for action."

"You can count on me when that time comes! But until then, darling, why don't you come here? You can have your old room for a few days, and I'll take good care of—"

"Thanks," Mick interrupted gently. "But I think it's best if I stay away from you and Dad for a while. I don't want to drag the whole family in on this, if I can help it."

After another pause, she sighed. "Oh, Michael!"

"I mean it, Mom," he said earnestly. "When I've sorted things out in my own mind, maybe there will be something for us all to do. For now, you stay there and I'll stay here. Let Rob play errand boy in the meantime. He's eating up the excitement."

Beth Piper gave an unladylike snort. "That boy never did have his priorities straight." Then, forcing herself to sound bright, she said, "Well, now, tell me about your telephone girl, dear. Any woman who presumes to take care of you has got to prove her worthiness to *me* before she starts making claims on my son."

"You would approve wholeheartedly," he said, smiling.

"Is she sexy?"

"Mother," he warned, trying to sound dangerous in spite of the grin on his face.

"You can't blame me for asking. Rob said this one was a looker, but I don't trust his judgment. True love, is it?"

Mick laughed and wisely did not answer her question. Beth Piper had no qualms about invading personal territory, and could still make her grown children squirm. Mick preferred to keep his love life a secret from his family. It was safer that way. Unfortunately, he knew his silence on the subject occasionally prompted outrageous speculation that simply led to more questions. Before he got himself into trouble with Abby Vanderbine, standing just a few yards away, Mick said lightly, "I think it's time to say good-bye, Mother. Call again when you have more time to talk, all right?"

"Michael," she said fondly, "you still have a healthy dose of devilment in you."

"We both know where it came from."

"Yes, I suppose so." Beth's laugh disintegrated, though, and she hesitated. In a different tone, she said, "Michael . . ."

"Yes?"

"This whole affair really hurts me, darling."

Mick sucked in a breath and didn't answer. He looked down at the floor.

Uncharacteristically, there was a quiver in her voice when she continued, the kind of crack that stabbed straight into Mick's heart. She said, "I—I *hate* to see you suffering. You, of all people."

"It's okay, Mom."

"It *isn't* okay! You've been through so much already, and just when you're getting back to—well, it's *horrible*, that's all, and *unfair* and—" She stopped herself, choking back her emotion. When she could speak again, she added heatedly, "I would do *anything* to make things turn out all right for you, darling!"

Mick ground his teeth. Beth Piper was the strongest woman he knew. She never cracked under pressure, never broke down in the face of adversity. In fact, Mick had never seen his mother cry until Laura's funeral. Now, hearing her strangled voice trail off was almost more than he could stand.

"I'm sorry," she said, her voice too high and strained and rushed. "I don't mean to—oh, never mind." She tried to laugh, but it was unsteady and weak. "I've got to go. Good-bye, good-bye! I'll call again when I can act like an adult!"

Mick heard the line click, and then the dial tone whined in his ear.

He turned and slammed the receiver back into the unit. Without a word to Abby, he went out through the patio doors and into the cool air of the evening.

Abby stared after Mick in wonderment. One moment he had been laughing on the telephone with his mother, and in the next instant he was storming outside to be alone. Mystified, she followed.

"Mick?"

He stood on the edge of the patio with his back to her. His shoulders were hunched, and he had thrust both his hands down into the front pockets of his jeans. He swore once, succinctly.

Abby hesitated, hearing the real anger in his voice this time. Tentatively, she asked, "Is there anything I can do?"

"No, dammit," he shouted suddenly, not turning around. "There's not a damn thing *anyone* can do! Christmas! How am I supposed to stand around waiting for some strangers to rescue me? God, Abby, this is more than I can take!"

Abby went out into the fading light toward him, though she paused while she was still several yards away, clasping her hands together. "I know it's difficult for you. But it can't go on much longer. The FBI is bound to make some progress by tomorrow, and—"

"Tomorrow?" he exploded, his body reverberating with the force of his anger. "How am I supposed to get through another night like this? Rob is a panicked madman—and my mother, who hasn't so much as uttered a whimper in the last eight years, is sitting at home and—"

Abby touched him. She put both her hands on his back to steady him and said gently, "They love you very much, you know. That's why they're upset. But if you let it get to you, Mick, you're only going to make things worse for them, too."

He was trembling. The frustration inside him had built up to such proportions that he could hardly keep it at bay any longer. Beneath her hands, his back was taut and almost shivering. He said, "I've never felt like running away before."

"You're not going to run away," Abby replied, sure of herself.

"But I *want* to. I want to clear out and forget about everything that's happened!" He spun around then and grabbed her by the shoulders. His eyes were fiery, and his face was tense and very white. Gripping her tightly, he snapped, "I wish I could get far away and pretend this has never happened!"

"But you won't."

He released her abruptly. "No, dammit, I won't. If it were only me, I'd get into the truck and keep driving until I hit the Pacific Ocean. But the rest of them—"

"Your family understands, Mick."

"I wish they wouldn't be so damned understanding! I wish they'd quit thinking I'm Prince Valiant for once and—and just let me fight this thing on my own! But they're constantly tugging on me, don't you see? I wish to God they'd just turn their backs and say, 'Tough luck, Mick. See you when it's all over.'"

"We're all feeling helpless."

"At least *you've* got something to do! You can answer the phone and make yourself useful—why you're still here, I can't imagine, but—"

"I wanted to stay."

He glared at her and demanded, "Why?"

"Because," she retorted childishly. "I wanted to, that's all. I thought I could help."

"You can. You have. Everybody has something to do but me!" He raked his fingers back through his hair. "Being cooped up in jail was bad enough, but hanging around here watching you all day— How am I supposed to— Oh, the hell with it!"

Much more steadily than she was feeling, Abby said, "I think you need to let it out, Mick."

"Let what out?"

"Your anger, the frustration. Keeping everything inside yourself like this—it's too difficult. You can't be Mr. Nice Guy all the time."

"Doesn't that scare you?"

"Why?"

He threw his arm wide. "We're all alone out here, Miss Sophisticate. What if I turn into a raving lunatic tonight?"

"It will probably be good for you to let some of those emotions out, as a matter of fact. Otherwise, you might *really* snap."

Mick didn't smile. He looked grim. "And what happens to you if I go off the deep end?"

Bravely, Abby said, "Nothing will happen to me unless I want it to."

Mick's gaze flickered. He waited for her to explain.

Quietly, Abby said, "I'm not completely sure why I stayed, Mick. But it wasn't to play your secretary or your nursemaid."

"What other role did you have in mind?"

"I—I'm not sure." Abby steadied herself with an effort. She had never talked with a man this way before—so directly, so honestly. She wasn't sure she liked doing it now, for that matter. It was definitely scary. She needed a moment to think, to be absolutely sure, and yet she could not bring the usual arguments into her brain. She admitted, "Maybe the other roles do scare me a little."

Suddenly, Mick said, "I think you'd better get your stuff together and clear out."

"Why?" she asked, startled.

"Before I—before things get out of hand," he said roughly, running his hand through his hair in exasperation. "I'm not myself tonight, and I can't be trusted. I'll call my mother back. You can stay with her, if you like and—" He stopped and almost choked. "What are you doing?"

Abby's fingers were trembling so violently that she could hardly manage the buttons. But the shirt parted finally, and she slipped it from her shoulders. She was acting foolishly, perhaps. But she wanted to give in to the impulse she had felt since the first time Mick had kissed her. It wasn't that he needed comfort, either. He was strong and electrifying, a desirable man with so many nice facets that she continued to discover. Yes, this was a man Abby wanted very much. She hugged the fabric to the front of her bra and turned to him with determination.

"Mick, I don't want to go stay with your mother."

His face wasn't quite blank. He glanced down at her

body and tried to control his reaction. "Abby," he warned when he could speak, "this isn't a good night to start any kind of meaningful relationship, believe me." He came to her swiftly, but halted just an arm's length away. He loomed there and said, "To begin with, I'd be a lousy lover just now. And your reasons for doing this are—they're not exactly what a man wants to—"

"I'm not feeling sorry for you," she intervened gently. "I'm thinking of myself now. It's impulsive, I know, but I want to—to make love with you."

He smiled a little. "You can hardly say the words without blushing."

"I'm not a brave woman, Mick."

"You're brave enough to carry off this—this—"

Abby smiled wanly. "A blushing striptease? Would you like me to do that?"

He laughed, but with a gleam of something different in his eyes. "Yes, I'd love it. But it would be a big mistake, don't you see? I think we—that under different circumstance, you and I could be— Damnation!" he said explosively. "Do you know what you're doing?"

She slipped out of her bra and laid it over the back of a patio chair. She could hardly believe herself. She was cool, so cool on the surface! Never had Abby Vanderbine acted so recklessly. Her breasts were bare, but shielded from his sight by the shirt she still clasped before her. With one hand, Abby began to unfasten the ponytail at the nape of her neck. She fumbled with the clip, and it slipped from her fingers and clattered on the concrete. Abby shook out her hair, and it fanned softly around her shoulders. She heard Mick inhale a sharp breath.

She looked at him. In a whisper, she said, "Yes, I know what I'm doing."

"Do you know what you may very well get?"

Steadily, though her heart was pounding, she said, "I don't expect you to be a textbook lover, if that's what you mean. After all, you spent the day taking out your frustration on a basketball. But with me . . . I think you'll be a little gentler than you were with the ball."

"Maybe so," he murmured, coming to her in two quick strides.

He caught her by her arms and pulled her into his body. The heat was immediate. Through their jeans, Abby could feel that Mick was already prepared to make passionate love. He was frowning, struggling with his own concern for her, she knew. His eyes bore deeply into hers, seeking the proof that she was honest with him.

He said quietly. "You aren't afraid, are you?"

She didn't answer but laid her hands on his chest and felt Mick's heart slam beneath his shirt. Her own pulse accelerated, and her hands began to tremble. Softly, she urged, "Kiss me, Mick."

He hovered there for a split second, hesitating. Abby was tormented by the suggestion that he might let go and walk away from her. Then, slowly, he bent and took her mouth with his. His lips tasted like liquid fire, searing an imprint on her sensitive mouth. Almost too quickly, he forced his tongue between her teeth, too swept away to restrain himself. He wrapped one arm expertly around her waist, snaring her against his lean frame and making no secret of his aroused state.

He demanded that she respond, also. He gathered her up hard against him and quickly eased his knee between her thighs. Abby capitulated almost eagerly, delighting in the feel of his rough assertion. The sensual power of his kiss was intoxicating. He thrust his tongue into the depths of her mouth, grasping the long hair at the back of her neck and holding her head inescapably.

She held him recklessly, too, weaving her fingertips into his thick dark hair and pouring her soul into the kiss. She had wanted to kiss him like this ever since their first morning together, and she matched her mouth to his fervently. Mick groaned deep in his throat, as a keen rush of desire welled inside her. This was too exciting, too exhilarating. She could hardly stand up.

He released her mouth, and Abby gasped for breath. She felt light-headed, and her heart was racing out of control. She threw her head back, exposing her throat to him. Mick kissed her neck, closing his teeth very gently on her skin. With one hand, he pulled the shirt away from her breasts. He found her nipple with his thumb, cupping the weight of her breast tightly in his hand.

"Abby, love, this is crazy." His voice was a muffled rasp against her flesh. "I don't want to hurt you."

"You won't hurt me," she coaxed, petting him, holding his head to her. "I'm a big girl who can take care of herself, Mick."

"I can't stop this now. Come inside with me. Now, Abby. I can't wait any longer."

Somehow he took her into the house. Abby later wouldn't remember how, exactly. She only knew that in a matter of heartbeats they were before the fire in the den, breathlessly undressing each other and speaking in nonsensical whispers.

Mick's body was strong and golden, finely honed, yet incredibly masculine. He got out of his shirt and was hardly patient enough to allow Abby to peel him out of his jeans. They were in each other's arms soon enough, relishing the sensations of skin against skin.

Abby moaned and wound her arms around Mick's shoulders. She pressed her mouth to his. Her breasts were softly crushed against the hard muscle of his chest. She

explored his back with her hands, as if to memorize every
detail, and smoothed down to the lean curve of his but-
tocks. She pulled him close, obliterating the barest space
between their bodies. She ground her hipbones into his,
feeling brave and wanton.

All the time, Mick was exploring just as swiftly, with
just as much turmoil. He pressed her down onto the rug,
taking time to rip a cushion from the sofa for her head.
With firm hands, he caressed her body, going down her
belly to her thighs and back up again, enjoying each
curve. His eyes glowed as he admired her, bringing yet
another hot blush to Abby's cheeks.

"You're lovely," he said, hushed and husky. "Who'd
ever mistake you for a stuffy society dame? You're en-
chanting, Abby love."

He found her breasts with his mouth then, flicking
the nipple with his tongue until she cried out, and then
sucking until a languorous tide overwhelmed her entirely.

"I want you *now*," he murmured raggedly when her
moan died away. "Next time, Abby—next time I'll make
it good for you, but please . . ."

It was too fast, but so good that Abby couldn't imagine
anything better. The ferocity with which Mick took her,
the heat of his passion and the intensity of his delicious
thrust was more than she could stand. She called out and
tried to slow him down, to make him savor the beauty
of the moment.

No use. Mick was nearly over the edge. All the pent-
up frustration within him boiled to the surface. He was
powerful and insistent, masterful and hungry. They struggled briefly, straining against each other with awkward
unfamiliarity before a joyous moment came when they
finally moved fluidly, gracefully, as one. Fire turned to
embers, warm and just as beautiful. Gradually, though,

a wild woman within Abby began to take over. She felt as if she was propelled by primitive instinct, and she could not have stopped herself from responding if she had wanted to. Their breathing became synchronized, their exclamations simultaneous. The rhythm of their coupling turning rampant until that exquisite moment, the zenith of their mutual pleasure, burst in an explosion of sensual satisfaction.

Abby hugged Mick against herself and felt the tension leave his body as though borne away on an evening breeze. In her arms, he turned gentle, kissing her mouth with tenderness.

"Dear Abby," he said, so softly that she could barely discern the words. "What would I have done if you hadn't walked into my life?"

CHAPTER TEN

ABBY AWOKE GRADUALLY and became aware of Mick's body, his breathing, his heartbeat, at the same time remembering her own. If it was possible to become part of another person in a matter of days, Abby was sure she had done it. They were cuddled up together in Mick's bed, legs entwined, noses almost touching. Abby smiled as the memory of their night together opened within her mind like warm, budding blossoms. She opened her eyes and Mick was smiling, too. There was a shadow in his eyes, though.

He didn't speak. He touched the smallest of kisses on her mouth, and then slowly, tenderly, used his fingertip to massage the kiss into her lips.

And Abby, her throat almost too tight to allow speech, slipped both her hands to his face, memorizing the angles and planes with her fingers and smoothing the crinkle

129

between his brows. He was worried already. Seeing that, she whispered, "Don't apologize."

"How did you know I was going to?"

She smiled. "I've gotten to know you very quickly."

He sighed, closed his eyes, and the crinkle deepened. "I am sorry for that, Abby. I should have—this was too soon."

"This," she murmured, caressing his shoulders and then his chest, "was hardly soon enough. No regrets. Not for me, at least."

He gathered her into a hug, one that was surprisingly fierce. "Nor for me, either. Except that I'm not usually the kind who can jump into bed with someone without a lot of thinking beforehand."

"Maybe it's better that you didn't think," Abby said, holding him. She was glad he couldn't see her face for a moment, for the emotion in his embrace was evident to her. She melted closer to him and tried to say lightly, "You might have talked us both out of this, and then where would we be?"

"Lonesome and frustrated, but in our own beds at least," he said, sounding grim. He loosened his grip by inches and then eased up on one elbow above her, looking into her eyes for signs that she was merely being kind.

Abby smiled encouragingly and rested one hand on his chest. They regarded each other for a moment, and she said gently. "You've had enough frustration for a while, I think."

"I took it out on you," he said solemnly. "Did I hurt you?"

"Of course not." Playfully, she tugged at the thick hair at the back of his neck. "I loved every moment, you animal."

He smiled then and rolled over, pinning her beneath

him in the bed. The friction of their bare bodies was tantalizing and delicious. When she wrapped her arms around his neck, Mick cupped her shoulders and looked into her face. Ruefully, he explained, "I lost my head last night."

"Do you hear me complaining?"

"No, but—well, a lady hardly wants to be the nearest target for a man who's releasing his frustrations."

Sure of his answer, Abby asked, "Is that what I was? Somebody who got in your way at the time—"

"No, no," he said swiftly, holding her. "But I would have taken the time to—to do things right if I'd been thinking straight. Honestly, Abby, you're the kind of lady I've been—"

"Don't say any more," she intervened. She smiled, though she knew her mouth was probably trembling. "I know you're trying to explain things, but I think—well, maybe it's too early to talk like this."

He looked skeptical. "You're sure?"

She grinned. "No woman wants to be called a lady in bed. I think I'll wait to hear the speeches from you when you've got your act together, Mr. Piper."

Mick watched her eyes for signs of doubt. He sighed, then slipped down to kiss her throat very lightly. Murmuring, he said, "You're very kind. And generous and passionate and gentle. You're perfect, Abby love."

She released a shaky sigh as Mick's lips found the valley between her breasts. He traced a lazy circle there and brushed his nose along the curve of her breast. Finally, he closed his teeth around her nipple with erotic gentleness. The contact sent volts of excitement surging through her veins, and Abby hastily caught his head in her hands and held Mick off, gasping. When he looked up at her, his head tipped askance, Abby whispered, "You know, I—I've never been this way before, Mick, if it makes you feel better about—about what we're doing."

He smiled. "So we're both off the deep end?"

"Yes, a little." Abby struggled to explain herself, "Confused, but excited, I guess. And a little wild, too."

He tipped his head, looking amused. "That striptease last night was hard for you, wasn't it?"

"It should have been," Abby admitted, feeling her cheeks warm, "but it wasn't. That surprised me. With you, I'm braver and—and just different."

"Different?

Uncertainly, she said. "Ryan—that's the man I lived with for a couple of years—he and I were never so—so explosive as this. I enjoyed being with him, don't get me wrong, but not like this. The intensity that I felt last night with you was—well, you're not like him, that's all."

"I was angry last night."

"I don't mean that," she argued softly, avoiding his searching gaze. "Of course, last night the circumstances were—oh, what I mean is that when we first met, I felt—I wanted—I couldn't help—"

He grinned. "Feeling wicked lust for me?"

"Mick," she groaned, "you're embarrassing me again!"

He was laughing then, cuddling Abby and running his lips over her breasts, teasing her. "Mmmm. Don't be embarrassed. It's been the same for me, dearest Abby. I want to nibble every inch of you!"

She tried to struggle away from his sensual exploration. "Mick, please, if you don't stop that—hey, it makes me—that makes me crazy!"

"You've been driving *me* crazy since we met! Those impeccable good manners of yours and that starched suit and pretty high heels. I've wanted you right here in my bed since the first time I saw you. Remember how I kissed you on the picnic table? You should have seen the fantasy that was playing in my head. I wanted to do so much more on the table, and we'd known each other for half an hour! Now that you're here with me like this, I want everything."

"Ev-everything?"

He laughed at her immediately wary expression. "My dear Abby, first you torment me with your cool-as-ice routine, and now you're warm and tucked into my bed as if you've been with me for years. What do you expect? I want you all over again. And over and over."

"Oh, Mick."

"See?"

Abby smiled. "Oh, *Mick.*"

"Say it again," he prompted, dropping his voice to a husky murmur.

He took her mouth first and kissed her thoroughly, deeply, kindling her desire to the boiling point. Against her lips, he said, "Say it again."

"Oooh," Abby sighed. "Mick..."

The morning passed.

Empty stomachs finally drove them to get dressed and go downstairs, and they had been sitting at the kitchen table only ten minutes when the doorbell chimed.

"Let me get it," Mick said, pushing Abby back down into her chair. "I'm fed up with being protected."

"Mick—"

"Don't look so worried. I can't continue to do nothing, Abby, dear. Today starts the campaign."

Mick left her, and Abby slowly cleared their dishes and juice glasses off the table, thinking. She knew that Mick had been trying to do exactly as Rob Piper asked, but he couldn't continue to watch helplessly as his name and reputation went down the drain. Now Mick was ready to fight his own battles, and though she was afraid that he might get his feelings hurt, Abby was secretly glad that Mick had decided to act. Last night he had proven to himself and to her that he was a man of action.

He returned to the kitchen and behind him was Clay Calloway, dressed in a scruffy raincoat and carrying a battered briefcase. Clay looked tired, but glad to be among friends.

"Clay!" Abby exclaimed. "How nice to see you."

Clay's face split into a big grin when his eyes fell on Mick's houseguest, complete with her host's flannel shirt on her back. He greeted her like an old friend, grasping her hand. "'Morning, Abby. I see you're still in town."

"Oh, yes. I hate leaving a movie before it's over."

Mick asked, "What's going on, Clay?"

"Plenty," the lawyer said, and his expression changed, clouding with concern. "Mick, we've got a lot to talk about."

"I don't like the sound of that."

"You're going to like the details even less. Do I smell coffee?"

"It will be ready in just a minute," Abby said. "Do you want me to leave you two alone?"

"No," Mick said at once, pulling a kitchen chair out for Clay. "Let's hear it, old buddy. Are the cops getting ready to arrest me?"

"This is no joke," Clay retorted, and he took a seat, unbuttoning his raincoat. "Mick, I'm your friend, not just your lawyer. I don't like asking you some of these questions, and I hope you'll keep that in mind."

Mick's face was grave. "Okay, Calloway. What's going on?"

Clay got right to the point. "The cops are having trouble with this case, Mick. That's not unusual, since it's apparently a random kind of crime perpetrated against random victims by somebody who is clearly unbalanced. It's like looking for a needle in a haystack, and I don't envy them this case. You're their only halfway decent suspect, Mick, simply because they don't have anyone better in mind."

"They haven't given up looking for the real criminal, have they?"

"Not exactly, no. But they're devoting more and more time to the case against you, my friend. So far, all the evidence pointing to you is circumstantial. Their biggest problem up until now is that you didn't really have a motive for poisoning your own peanut butter."

"Up until now?" Mick repeated. "Uh-oh."

Clay nodded. "Have you seen the financial pages in the last couple of days?"

"No, the *Journal* is delivered to the office, and I haven't been over there yet. Why?"

"The stock of Piper's Peanut Butter is plunging."

Mick shook his head and sighed. "I guess that's to be expected. I can't blame stockholders for wanting to sell their stock before they lose their shirts."

"How about you?" Clay asked shrewdly. "Don't you own a lot of the stock in Pipers?"

"Sure. More than thirty percent now. You've been helping me to acquire it, Clay."

Abby returned to the table with cups and the sugar bowl. "If I'm allowed to listen, gentlemen, you're going to have to explain things carefully. What's this all about?"

Willingly, Mick said, "It's no big deal. I think I mentioned this once before to you. Over the last couple of years, my strategy has been to buy as much of the stock in Piper's Peanut Butter as I possibly could. I'd like to own the company outright, and the only way to do that is to buy up all the—"

He broke off as a thought connected in his brain. He jerked his attention to Clay and said, "Oh, hell. I think I understand now."

Clay nodded grimly. To Abby, he said, "You and I know that Mick isn't the kind of guy to ruin his own company. But let's imagine for a minute that he's not the Mick we know. If he wants to own the entire company himself, he needs to find a way to make everybody want to sell their shares. Even better, he might want the price to be low so he could buy it all up without too much of a financial strain on himself. After the bad publicity dies down, he could work doubly hard and make Piper's Peanut Butter a big success again, only this time he owns all of it."

"Wait a minute," Abby protested. "You mean that the FBI thinks Mick might have sabotaged the peanut butter so all the other stockholders would chicken out and sell their stock to him cheaply?"

"Exactly."

"But why would he buy stock in a company that's in such trouble?"

"Piper's Peanut Butter won't suffer forever because of this poisoning scare," Clay explained. "Mick will have a bad year probably, but the tax laws will be in his favor. Plenty of companies have bounced back from worse catastrophes in very little time. Right now, Piper's is an ad agency's dream."

Abby remembered the phone call she had received from an advertising agency in New York. Perhaps Mick's company wasn't in such bad shape after all. It was Mick himself who was in danger now.

"So," Mick said finally, "now I have a motive, I guess."

Clay nodded. "This morning the price of Piper's stock was at an all-time low, Mick. If you weren't in so much trouble, I'd suggest that you start buying like crazy."

"But that would make me look guilty as hell, right? You know, somebody with the FBI is pretty clever to have figured out a scheme like this."

Clay glanced at Abby, then away, and he reached for the sugar bowl. Toying with it, he said, "Actually, I think they had an informant."

"An informant!" Abby cried. "Who?"

Clay looked up at Mick, then back to Abby, and suddenly she knew. "Rob?"

Clay nodded. "I saw Rob this morning downtown at the diner where a few of us have coffee every morning. He was upset, let me tell you. Tears in his eyes!"

"He must have been an unwitting informant," Mick murmured.

"Unwilling anyway," Clay said.

"The FBI had practically broken into his house, he said. They had gotten him out of bed to question him, and he kind of—well, he let it slip that you've been wanting to own the company yourself for a long time. 'A burning ambition,' he called it, I think. But he was mortified when the FBI began to question him further on the subject. He didn't mean to implicate you, Mick. It just slipped out. He's more loyal to you than any natural brother could possibly be."

"Damn," Mick said, just as softly as before. He stared out the kitchen window and said, "This isn't good news, Clay."

"You're tellin' me, old buddy. Now the FBI is really motivated to find some hard evidence against you."

"Like what, for heaven's sake?" Abby demanded. "Fingerprints? A stray prescription for penicillin lying around somewhere?"

Clay nodded. "Anything. I beat it up here as fast as I could, but I bet they'll show up with a search warrant any minute."

"They searched the place already," Mick said. "The very first day while I was still at the office. They didn't find a thing."

"They'll try again. And again and again, if they have to. In addition to this motive thing, that insurance business looks pretty damning, too, Mick. All that coverage for an unlikely kind of lawsuit—it's too coincidental for the FBI's taste."

"Well?" Mick asked when silence had fallen. "What should I be doing, counselor? Packing for a trip to South America so I don't get framed?"

"No," said Clay, shaking his head. "We'll get you off the hook if you're innocent, Mick."

Abby had been about to pour hot coffee into their cups, when she suddenly jerked, splashing the table. "What do you mean, Clay? *If* he's innocent?"

"I—it was just a—"

"Great!" Abby snapped as anger surged within her. "Now your lawyer is starting to have doubts! I can't believe that—"

"Abby," Mick began, "it's okay."

"No, it's not," Clay said abruptly. His already red face was flushed. "I'm sorry, Mick, it just slipped out. I can't— I must be losing my touch or something. With all this evidence starting to pile up, it's getting tougher and tougher to find the loopholes for you."

"We don't need loopholes," Mick said sharply. "I *am*

innocent, and they've got to prove that I'm guilty before I get carted off to jail."

Looking like a sorrowful spaniel, Clay said, "I wish that our judicial system really worked that way, Mick, but it's—well, what's ahead for all of us is not going to be easy, you know."

"I know," Mick said gruffly.

"In the meantime," Clay suggested, leaning forward with his elbows on the table, "I think you'd better keep on doing what you've been doing. Don't go out, don't get involved, don't talk to the press. Just stay here and—well, let Abby take care of you."

Mick glanced up at Abby, but his eyes were distant and the color of cold slate, as if he wasn't thinking about her at all. He said firmly, "I can't make any promises, Clay."

Clay nodded understandingly. It seemed to Abby that he knew his friend pretty well, also. Mick was going to do as he pleased now, and Clay was not going to stop him. Perhaps flustered by the fact that he had upset Abby, Clay did not stay to drink his coffee. He made his excuses and quickly left the house. Standing at the front door, he told Mick to call him if the FBI showed up for another search.

Mick went back up to the kitchen with his hands thrust down into the pockets of his jeans. He didn't feel helpless anymore. He felt gloriously angry with the world.

"Abby," he said bluntly, "I need your help."

For a moment, she had looked very sad, but then she must have seen the look in his eyes. She sat up attentively, ready for action. "Sure," she said. "Name it."

"I'm going to make some phone calls and then I want

you to run some errands for me. Will you?"

"Of course. What do you have in mind?"

"I've been working on a mental list," he told her. He crossed to the cupboards under the telephone and pulled open the junk drawer to look for paper and pen. Over his shoulder, he said, "I'm the only one who really knows the chain of production for Piper's Peanut Butter. I know all the men who work in the plant, I know the drivers, and I know most of the grocery chains where the jars go. If I think about it hard enough, I should be able to figure out exactly whose hands those tainted jars passed through on their way to the victims. *I'm* the only one who can do that."

"I'll help," Abby said earnestly when he had turned around. "Just tell me what to do."

Mick studied her upturned face and determined eyes for a moment, and he felt his own expression soften. Inside, he felt a quick implosion—a combination of a lot of emotions coming together with a catalyst. Abby was lovely—all ovals and pastel colors with that corona of pale blond hair that felt like liquid sunshine in his hands. Her body was long-legged and curving and her skin smelled naturally like subtle flowers. Mick had long ago decided that her softness was a paradox, however. Last night he had felt her strength, her almost tensile willpower. She was everything a woman ought to be, he thought: gentle, yet impervious. Willing to help without asking questions.

Was it possible to hurt a woman like Abby Vander-bine? Perhaps.

She was just vulnerable enough to be—well, dangerous. A woman didn't yield to a man the way she had without experiencing the kind of emotional bond that Mick had denied himself for so long.

He should feel guilty, he supposed. He would be a louse if he used this fragile-strong woman and then shooed her out of his life when the crisis was passed. But Mick couldn't think about life after the current dilemma. Not yet, anyway. He didn't dare start hoping yet that his troubles might end and that he could rebuild his life. He couldn't think beyond the present.

"I want to help," she insisted gently.

Her eyes were full of light and her complexion still tinged with pink from their lovemaking. Mick decided that the urges he was feeling inside himself couldn't be completely wrong. For the first time in almost a decade, he was attracted to a woman, a *real* woman, who was more than mere flesh and blood. If she had wandered into his life at any other time, wouldn't he have felt the same way about her? Or was it the excitement of the company sabotage and the resulting trouble that was keeping him from thinking straight? Surely not. Surely under different circumstances, he might even have fallen in love with her.

"All right," he said, and smiled. He stopped listening to his conscience, for the sight of her patrician features bravely hardened for the fight to come was more appealing than he could withstand. "But first," he said, pulling her against himself, "I think you'd better kiss me."

She came willingly, eagerly, into his arms, but her natural shyness caught her up short. Mick had to be the one to slip his hand around the nape of her neck and tilt her face up to his. Her kiss was warm, though, and hesitantly sensual. Then she licked his tongue with her own and lingered to savor the deeper essence of his mouth. Her hands slid—perhaps unconsciously—up his chest until Mick almost writhed beneath her touch like a pet seeking caresses. His body betrayed his usually steady brain, and a blaze of desire filled his loins yet again. In response, Abby instinctively melted her slimness to his harder frame. She was his, and, with no coaxing, Mick knew he could have her then and there.

But she gave more than just sex, Mick thought dimly, even as their aroused kiss faded away into the merest contact. Abby gave her support, her soul, without questions. For that, a man had to be grateful.

He should also be careful.

Mick set her away from him gently, though his breathing was rapid. "Enough recreation," he said, feebly trying for a joke. "Let's get to work."

Abby slipped out of his arms with a lighthearted laugh and sketched a salute. "Right, Chief. Give me my orders and I'll stay out of your way."

Good as her word, she obediently kept her distance from him for the rest of the day. Mick knew he had to concentrate on his problems. He wisely tried to empty Abby's presence from his mind by sending her back to his office to pick up some blueprints of the plant. When she returned with those, he wrote out a list of questions for Frank, his plant foreman, to answer, and Abby delivered them. Under his orders, she waited until Frank had carefully written out responses to each one and then she returned to the house. She pored over the papers with him.

She was smart, too, thank heavens. Mick knew that he was looking for a needle in a haystack, all right, but as they wrote out endless lists and compared notes, he realized that Abby had caught on to his system easily. She doggedly followed the route of a single jar of peanut butter with him and even pointed out a mistake that Mick had made. He was thankful to have her on his side. It felt good to be working with her, and it seemed as if they were making some progress. His goal was to come up with a narrowed list of suspects.

To spoil his day, however, the FBI showed up. They had given his house only a cursory search the first time, it seemed, for three officers spent the entire afternoon tearing into everything that Mick owned. They emptied out the contents of his kitchen cupboards. They emptied containers of shampoo, toothpaste, and shaving cream. They shook out all the sheets, towels, and blankets in the closet. They even ripped up the wall-to-wall carpet in the basement game room. Abby's face was white and wide-eyed. She was sickened by the sight, he could see.

"I can't stand this," he said to her, grabbing her hand and dragging her out the patio doors. "Let's go out!"

He had left his basketball on the patio chairs, and without thinking, he picked it up and began to dribble, slamming the ball into the concrete. It felt good to hit something. He passed the ball to Abby, and she caught it instinctively.

"C'mon," he urged. "One on one, Vanderbine!"

Abby laughed weakly and nearly declined, but then she bounced the ball inexpertly a couple of times—and accepted his challenge. She dribbled—not badly, in fact— over to the basket, where she faked, jumped, and then shot the ball. Missed. Mick leaped and caught it easily, cutting around her body and dribbling fast. He spun, shot, and the ball hit the rim, ricocheted, and swished through the net. He crowed with delight.

Getting into the spirit of the game, Abby caught the ball, elbowed him in the ribs to stifle his jubilation, and then she raced away from him, her hair streaming, her voice bubbling in laughter. Watching her go, Mick felt something quick and painful tear at his belly. He *was* falling in love with her.

The dawning realization spoiled Mick's concentration. He played badly, watching Abby and trying to succeed completely in putting the police out of his mind. While the FBI ripped his house to pieces, they played basketball on the patio, running, shooting, shoving, gasping. They played hard, too. Abby wasn't very good, of course, but she made him work for his points. And she wasn't above cheating now and then to punish him for his fancy footwork.

They played until it was starting to get dark, until the FBI cleared out and left them alone. Mick wanted to take Abby straight back to the shower. He wanted to bathe her lithe body himself, smoothing soapy lather all over her bare skin until he couldn't stand it. He wanted to pat her dry and take her to bed.

But she was hungry, she claimed, and she playfully fended him off. They ended up making dinner together and sitting on the patio until darkness came. Mick couldn't remember what they talked about. He absorbed every detail of her face, her laugh, her gestures, however. He was in love with her already.

The telephone rang after dinner, though, interrupting their peace and bringing them inside. Mick picked up the receiver while Abby measured coffee.

The male voice on the other end of the line was polite, but gruff. "I'm trying to track down Miss Abigail Vanderbine, please. Can she be found at this number?"

"Certainly," Mick said, and he handed over the receiver as though it was a hot potato. There were some voices with which a man didn't argue. This one sounded very possessive. Mick suspected that the voice was no other than Abby's father. He was too curious to give Abby any privacy, so he puttered with their cups and listened shamelessly.

"Hello, Father," she said coolly when the voice had identified himself. "How are you?"

Her father must have answered succinctly, and then he proceeded to deliver a lecture. Abby's face was controlled, not smiling. She was the cool, sophisticated lady again.

"Yes," Abby said when the lecture concluded and two small dots of pink appeared on her cheeks. "Yes, Father."

A moment later, she said hotly, "I can take care of myself!"

Evidently, her father spoke again. Then, even more angry, Abby snapped, "I've grown up since then, I'll have you know! I'm not being taken for a ride! No, Father, he is *not* a maniac! . . . I *know,* that's all!"

Mick glanced at her, one eyebrow raised. Abby immediately flushed even redder and said hastily into the telephone, "I'll get back when I get back, and that's all I can tell you. I can't promise about two nights from now. Look, I came because you sent me, remember? And I'm sure the magazine will survive without me for a little while longer! Good-bye, Father!"

She banged the phone down and stood for a moment, trembling.

"Well," Mick said, dunking her teabag with care. "What was that all about?"

"Nothing."

"It sounded like Dad is worried about your safety."

Abby tried to laugh. "I can't figure him out sometimes! Overly protective one day, but tossing me out into the cold, cruel world the next! Yes, he's afraid you're holding me hostage or something."

"Am I?" Mick asked slowly.

Abby drew a sharp breath. "Of course not. I just—I just thought I'd stay a little longer. They don't need me back in Chicago."

"What was the stuff about two nights from now?"

"Nothing, nothing," she said hastily. "Mother's having a dinner party, and she wants me to meet the guests, that's all. She does that kind of thing all the time lately—looking for a husband for me, I mean. It's embarrassing, and I don't mind missing the evening at all. And Father just wants me to get under his wing again."

"Sounds like they care about you."

Abby looked up at him, and she had caught her lower lip between her teeth in an expression that was too quick to be calculated. Mick suspected that her mouth was trembling, and something turned over inside his chest at that realization. He said, "A lot of people care about you, Dear Abby."

Her blue eyes widened, filled with puzzlement and—briefly—something that looked like hope. She was silent for a long time, though, unable to ask the questions that nine out of ten other women would surely have asked.

The look on her face could ruin a man, he thought. It drove every iota of sense out of his brain. He touched her arm with his fingertips, cupping her slender elbow in the palm of his hand. He couldn't look into her face anymore. "Abby," he said, "I have no right to ask you to stay with me. Lord knows I haven't got anything to offer you but a big chance of getting hurt, but—"

"Don't, Mick."

"Don't what?"

"Try making promises. I don't need any," she said, though the tremor he felt in her arm suggested that she wasn't absolutely convinced of that statement. In a rush, she said, "A man in your present position—well, I'd be a wishful thinker to imagine that you're capable of making any kind of important decisions about yourself. So just don't try."

"I don't like to think that I'm too addle-brained at the moment to—"

"You're not. But you don't need any extra pressure, do you? I just want to give you . . . some companionship, I guess."

It was far too late to be having this discussion, but here was Abby, ready to tuck both their feelings on a shelf like a good book she was saving to read on just the right rainy night. She was a plucky thing, he decided. And very smart.

It was her elusive vulnerability that nagged him, though. Abby wanted to pretend that she was stronger than she really was. She could go for hours looking cool as a cucumber, but then something brought a blush to her cheeks or made her drop her eyelashes to hide her true feelings. This was a woman who wouldn't take a one-night or one-week stand lightly. This was a woman who needed love, not sex. Still, her look was direct and completely lacking in fear. She trusted him, he realized. And the pang in his chest tightened at the thought.

Mick drew her closer, needing the warmth of her body next to his just then. "What do *you* want, Abby? What would you like to have for yourself?"

And she smiled up at him, winding her arms around his neck. Without hesitation, she said, "Another night like last night. Nothing less, nothing more."

CHAPTER ELEVEN

ABBY WOKE THE FOLLOWING MORNING with her father's words ringing in her ears.

"You're playing hooky," he had said on the telephone. "Either that, or you're back to playing journalistic detective. It's time to come home, Abigail."

She had refused. She wanted to stay with Mick. There was no doubt in her mind why she had chosen to remain in his house. She was in love with him, pure and simple. How could she have fallen hard for a man as sensitive and determinedly optimistic as Mick? He also happened to be the kind of lover that women daydream about. She couldn't tear herself away from him now that she had discovered him.

And that was out of character for Abby. She had dashed headlong into a relationship with a man before she had completely sorted out her feelings, and certainly before *he* had! Poor Mick had enough on his mind without adding women problems to the list. He didn't need the added pressure of making any kind of emotional commitment to her, even though Abby was aching for just that. She couldn't urge him to say these things yet, though. It would be cruel.

So Abby had allowed herself the pleasures of an intimate relationship before they could establish their feelings for each other. She knew Mick cared for her. She only hoped that he cared as deeply as she did for him. She eased over onto her back and reached for him.

Then she sat up abruptly. His side of the bed was cool, and he had disappeared. Mick was gone.

She grabbed yet another of his shirts out of his closet and went to look for him.

He was sitting at the kitchen table, wearing his jeans and nothing else, with sheets and sheets of paper scattered in front of him, a pen clenched in his hand and a distracted frown creasing his forehead. How long he had been working there, Abby couldn't guess. Even though there was no music playing for once, he didn't hear her enter the room.

Rather than startle him, she let Mick see her before she bent to brush a kiss across his temple. He smiled up at her at once and caught her hand quickly. "Morning."

"Hi," she said, breathless from the effects of his smoke-gray gaze. One smoldery look from Mick was all it took to make Abby's heart lift. When he pulled her into his lap, she found the perfect niche there, as though they'd been a couple for years. It felt good to hold him.

She instinctively touched his face, smiling. "Have you been up all night?"

He grinned, lazy-eyed. "Do I look that bad?"

"No," she said softly, giving him a brief, warm kiss

on his mouth. Against his lips, she murmured, "You look wonderful to me."

He pulled her close then, winding one strong arm around her waist and drawing her inexorably into his chest. His mouth caught hers quickly, searing and delicious. As their lips melted together, then fused in the heat of unspoken longing, Abby felt her pulse go tearing out of control. Sweet surrender was never calm no matter how hard she tried to make it look that way. In his throat, Mick gave a sated kind of groan. His other hand found its way under the tail of the shirt she was wearing, and then she felt him caress her bare back. Her own softer moan of pleasure echoed his.

All mornings should be like this, Abby thought dreamily. Lazy and exciting all at once, full of promise and sensual pleasures. She almost said the words that came to her mind with the swiftness of a springtime breeze. She almost whispered them then and there: *I love you*.

The strength of his body, the heat of his passion, the steady thump of his heart . . . Vividly, Abby recalled the gentle lovemaking they had shared the night before. Mick had forgotten his anger and had proved to be a tender, absorbed lover, savoring each caress, each moment, until the final flames of passion grew into the flash and lingering fire of ecstasy.

He broke the kiss first, if unwillingly. Abby eased away, her palms on his chest. She found him looking deeply into her eyes, as if making a telepathic connection.

Whatever he saw there made him smile and shake his head ruefully. He said, "I wish we'd had more time, Dear Abby."

"It's been too fast, hasn't it?"

"Much too fast. And I haven't been exactly devoting

my full attention to your—"

"Don't," she gently interrupted his apology. Somehow, postponing the verbal part of their sudden intimacy seemed the safest avenue. She brushed his hair back from his forehead with her fingertips. "When I need a speech from you, Mr. Piper, I'll ask for it."

His smile appeared once more, almost genuine. "That's a deal."

She smiled, too, and tried to sound cheery. "In the meantime, tell me what forced you out of bed so early. Did I steal the covers?"

"I couldn't sleep, but it had nothing to do with you," he explained, caressing her thigh. "I found that if I let myself start to think about you, I wanted to wake you up and start all over again. And when I started thinking about the company—well, I had to get up."

Abby reached for one of the papers he had been writing on. "So what's this? Have you made any progress?"

"I think so. I've got a list of all possible suspects— everyone who could have come in contact with the two batches of peanut butter that were affected."

"Two batches?"

"Right." Mick linked his hands loosely around her hipbone and explained. "I started checking on files. The penicillin must have been added to the peanut butter on two separate occasions."

"I see," Abby murmured, remaining on his lap and glancing down through the list of perhaps forty names. "Who are these people?"

"Mostly employees, I'm sorry to say. The night shift. And a few truckers who might have had access to the stuff. Here." He indicated two names on the list. "This guy is the night watchman, and this is the man who cleans up at night."

"Hmm." Abby read a few of the names. Thinking aloud, she asked, "Is the plant locked at night?"

"Sure. Always."

"Who has keys?"

He pointed again. "The names with asterisks, see?"

Abby nodded, trying to study Mick's work with the practiced eye of a former investigative reporter. Perhaps he had missed something she could find. Casually, she asked, "How about members of your family?"

"What about them?"

"Do you ever give keys to the plant to any of them?"

"Well, sure, but I hardly think they're suspects."

Abby smiled playfully and handed him the pen with a flourish. "If you are making a list of everybody who could have had access to the plant, you'd better make it a *complete* list. That includes your sister, right? She brings the bread deliveries. Who else?"

"Abby—" he began, protesting.

"I'm not suggesting that your sister did it," Abby said easily, though her pulse increased as she said so. "Someone might have gotten a key from her somehow, though, couldn't they? Without her knowing about it?"

Giving in unwillingly, Mick took the pen. He sent Abby a grim sort of smile. "Okay, Miss Vanderbine, have it your way. We'll add my sister to the list."

"Who else has keys?" she asked as he printed the name, using her thigh as a desk. "Your father?"

"Nope."

"Rob?"

Perhaps Mick heard something in her too-casual tone, for he looked directly into her eyes and didn't speak.

"Well?" Abby asked, trying to keep her face expressionless in spite of the way her chest hurt suddenly. "What about Rob?"

"What about him?"

"Does he have a key?"

"I don't know," Mick said stubbornly. There was a new edge in his voice. He looked away, throwing the pen onto the table.

"I may be speaking out of turn," Abby said before she could stop herself. Her breath was locked tightly in her throat, but she plunged ahead. "And you know Rob better than I do, certainly, but . . ."

"But what?" Mick asked curtly, his brows dangerously drawn together.

Abby edged off his lap and stood up nervously, gathering his oversized shirt around her otherwise bare body. "Well, I can't help noticing that Rob's been very interested in all the proceedings around here."

"Of course he has. He cares about how this thing turns out."

Nervous, Abby glided away from him. She said doggedly, "He's been at your side from the start, I know, but I—I can't help feeling a little suspicious, Mick. He was pumping you for information the day you were released by the FBI. He was also the one who accidentally let it slip to the authorities about your insurance coverage, not to mention your plans to buy up all the Piper stock you could lay your hands on—"

"Hold it. Are you saying that *Rob* is trying to frame me?"

Quickly, Abby turned around to face him. She was afraid suddenly. The incredulous tone he used was only a sham. He was angry. "No, no, no. I'm not saying that, Mick. I only meant that—"

"That's exactly what you're saying, isn't it?" he demanded, and a fiery light suddenly leaped into his eyes. With sarcasm, he said, "You think that Rob—who is practically my brother—has cooked up a very elaborate plan to ruin me?"

"Maybe not to ruin you," Abby argued gently. "But he's certainly got a grudge against you."

"Rob?" Mick retorted in amazement, staring at her from the table. "A *grudge?*"

Gathering her courage, Abby lifted her chin and insisted, "Yes, Mick, a grudge. And I can see why, too. You're perfect. You're smart and popular and successful and attractive and fun—all the things Rob would like to be. His distillery is having financial problems, right? He'd like to get his hand into Piper's Peanut Butter because he thinks he can do a better job of running the company than you can. You're having too much fun with your business, in his view. He wants you to get serious about making money."

Mick lunged out of his chair and wheeled away from Abby, as though he didn't trust himself to be near her. "That's nonsense."

"Is it? You told me the first day we met that Rob is a cutthroat businessman. He's been pressuring you to knuckle down and make huge profits out of peanut butter, hasn't he? Your style is too laid back for him." Abby realized that her hands were trembling, and she placed them flat on the cool counter. "You're such a nice guy, Mick—but I never thought your niceness was naiveté. Rob is *jealous* of you!"

"Jealous!" he exploded, stopped still and staring. "Over what?"

"Over lots of things. Business, your family. And—"

"And what?"

"You know as well as I do."

"Tell me anyway," he insisted, his voice almost as dangerous as a growl.

"Your wife," Abby said flatly. "He's jealous over Laura."

"That's ridiculous!" he snapped, going rapidly to the patio doors and bracing both his hands on the glass. "How could he be—for godsake, Abby, do you know how long Laura has been gone?"

"Yes, eight years. Eight years is a long time to have a pot of jealousy simmering, Mick. Rob has had almost a decade to let his anger get stronger and stronger."

"Ridiculous!" Mick repeated harshly.

"Maybe so. But," Abby persisted, holding her ground, "I think he wants to punish you for taking Laura away from him a long time ago, and I think he wants to prove that he's a better businessman than you are, too, by getting control of Piper's Peanut Butter. He wants to run the company himself."

"No."

"I bet you he's calling his stockbroker today!" Abby cried. "He's probably going to buy up as many cheap shares of Piper's Peanut Butter as he can get—all in the guise of helping out his poor beleaguered cousin."

"Stop it," Mick snapped.

"I will," Abby promised desperately, her voice rising to match his. "But not before—"

"I mean it, Abby!"

Rushing, she pleaded, "Mick, for once take a realistic look at this family loyalty of yours! Ever since I got here I've been hearing about the tightly knit Piper family— one for all and all for one! It's admirable, and I wish my family were half as close as yours! But, Mick, please, *please* take a minute and look at the situation. Look at the evidence!"

"This is absolute fiction! The FBI hasn't so much as suggested the possibility that Rob—"

"Of course not! What Rob has done should only be apparent to his family—the ones who will never turn him in. Besides, he's covered up his actions by those melodramatic emotional displays of his! Mick, he's tricked the FBI and he has completely snowed your family, all the while sneaking bits of incriminating evidence against you for—"

"That's enough!"

Abby fell silent, trembling. Inside, she felt suddenly nauseated. Her heart was pounding, and her hands felt clammy as she looked at Mick.

He was transformed. His face was white and taut with anger, his jaw clenched, his eyes flat and colorless. In his shoulders and arms, the tendons shivered under the surface of his skin with the pent-up tension. His hands were balled into fists. "I've heard enough," he said, voice cold as stone.

Staring, Abby said breathlessly, "I—I'm sorry."

"Save it," he snapped. "I've got very little left in life right now outside of my family, so you can just lay off them."

"Mick, I didn't mean—"

"You meant exactly what you said, Miss Vanderbine."

"Mick—"

"I've had a hard time figuring out why a woman like you would want to hang around a hick town and watch a hillbilly company go down the drain. Have you enjoyed your little slice of small-town life?" he demanded. "Aren't you satisfied with what you've seen and done without wanting to drag your big-city ideas into our lives? Maybe families rat on each other where you come from, Miss Epicurean, but around here—"

"You've lost your sense of perspective!"

"But *you* wouldn't!" Mick shouted. "I'm sure you've

got a crystal-clear vision when it comes to—"

"I'm sorry if I hurt you," Abby cried out. "And dammit, I *hope* that I'm wrong about Rob!"

"Why? Why should you care who is behind the sabotage? I'll bet you've been hoping all along that it *was* me, just so you could get some kind of thrill by sleeping with a poisoner! Is that it? You hung around here for kicks, right? That's what jet-set bitches do these days, don't they? Now you've decided it's not so exciting to—"

"Now I've heard enough," Abby shouted, clutching the counter to keep from running at him. She wasn't sure if she wanted to hit Mick or hug him, kiss him, hold him. "I've hurt your feelings, and for that—I'm sorry, Mick. I thought we—that you and I had— Oh, hell, I've done it now, haven't I?" She put her face into her hands and prayed that she wasn't going to cry.

"I'm not in the mood for tears, so don't try that tactic."

Abby tore her hands away and glared at him. "When I cry, it will be for a damned good reason, and in the privacy of my own home. I'm leaving."

"To cry? I doubt it. Probably because you're bored now with—"

"Be quiet, Mick," said Abby over her shoulder, already hurrying for the doorway and hugging his shirt around her, "before you make me think you really are as naive as you pretend to be!"

CHAPTER TWELVE

ABBY ARRIVED IN CHICAGO by midafternoon. She took a cab directly to her still-new apartment, got off the elevator, unlocked her door, walked straight through to the bedroom, and then fell across her bed and burst into sobs.

She had been horribly cruel. She had not only hurt Mick terribly, but she had ruined any possible chances of enjoying his friendship once he got his life back into order. It didn't matter that her theory about Rob was totally plausible; Mick's fidelity to his family was fierce and strong. No doubt he hated her now.

Abby cried for Mick, and she cried for herself. She hadn't shed a single tear over Ryan, but now she let her emotions pour out of her in great, gushing sobs.

However, it wouldn't do for a Vanderbine to admit utter dejection.

In time, Abby roused herself and began to move around her apartment, opening windows, defrosting a meal for herself, settling in once more. That night she stared dully at her empty bedroom, trying to put the memories of Mick Piper out of her mind. The unadorned walls of the room suddenly reminded her of Mick's equally stark home.

Abby had only lived in her apartment for a few weeks, and she hadn't taken the time to decorate and furnish the place properly. Just looking at the unfinished room made Abby think of a lonely man in his half-completed house. How was he? Had he eaten properly? Had the FBI returned to torment him? Mick's tenacious loyalty to his family was unswerving. And Abby had tried to take away the one kind of support Mick needed most. His family.

Abby had never felt so far from love.

Suddenly, she wanted to hear her mother's voice. Almost without thinking, she pulled the bedside telephone closer and dialed in the darkness.

"Sweetheart, you're back!" Mother cried, stifling a yawn. "Perfect! That means you'll be coming to dinner tomorrow night, after all."

"Mom, please," Abby begged. "I don't—"

"Your father and I won't take no for an answer," she blithely interrupted. "We've missed you very much, and we want to hear all about what happened—but save it for when I'm awake enough to listen. Come at seven for cocktails, all right?"

"Mother, I—"

"I'm tired now, sweetheart. Let me go to sleep, and I'll see you at dinner."

Abby hung up resignedly. If she had expected to be welcomed warmly back into the family fold, she was disappointed. The Vanderbines would not rally around one of their number the way the Piper clan might.

Mick stayed on her mind all night and all during the following day. Abby was even tempted to telephone him several times, but she was afraid to try apologizing. He had been so angry when they parted! Abby wished that she had the last week to live over again.

Later, she dressed herself in a simple green silk sheath—the same color, she noted ruefully, as the blossoming apple trees in Blue Creek, West Virginia. Tonight she had to play a Vanderbine, though. She fixed her hair, applied rather too much makeup, put on her best pearl earrings, and took a cab to her parents' lakeview home— the Vanderbine ancestral palace.

There was no longer a butler in the Vanderbine's employ, but Joanna, the new and nervous maid, opened the door for Abby, clumsily took her wrap, and disappeared. Abby found her parents in the solarium with a young couple that had been invited to dinner, and a man who was an old family friend by the name of Raymond O'Donnell, whom Abby suspected was the latest in a long line of men that her mother scrounged up as potential sons-in-law. It didn't take long for anyone to realize that Raymond had been a poor choice. He was a bore, talking about pension funds over cocktails. At least he didn't have romance on his mind. He paid more attention to Abby's father than anyone else.

The other couple that Mother had invited was interesting, however. Abby had once met the woman—a distant cousin of the Vanderbine clan who made her living as an etiquette columnist for various newspapers. The man was a hulkingly handsome former football player by the name of Lazurnovich. Though they looked like they might have each come from a separate universe, Grace and Luke Lazurnovich had been recently married, and they were obviously in the throes of love. Grace teasingly referred to her husband by his football nickname, "Laser," and they visibly enjoyed ribbing each other. They laughed a lot. All the while, they communicated the obvious message that they could hardly wait to be alone together. Just being around such happy lovers gave Abby a headache.

"Sweetheart," Abby's mother said when the fish course had been hastily served by a frightened Joanna, and the dinner conversation waned, "why don't you tell us about your time in Kentucky?"

"It was West Virginia, Mother."

Father, pouring wine for Grace Lazurnovich, said, "Abigail has been involved with that fellow who was putting drugs into peanut butter."

"He did not put the drugs into the peanut butter himself, Father," Abby snapped with too much force, ready to do battle.

"How interesting," said Grace, who was clearly a master at steering table conversation away from touchy issues. "Did you enjoy West Virginia?"

"Never mind about the state," Mother said, looking impish. "I saw photographs of that Piper fellow in tonight's newspaper. Such a Heathcliff type! Did he chase you across the moors, Abigail? Or don't they have moors in West Virginia?"

"He didn't chase me," Abby said, knowing full well that she was blushing. "And he was more like Huckleberry Finn than Heathcliff! Hardly worth the chase."

Across the table Abby unconsciously met the steady, incurious gaze of Luke Lazurnovich. She had the uncanny feeling that Luke knew exactly how she felt about Huckleberry Finn. He didn't say a word, however.

"Well," said her father after a dignified *haarumph.* "It's comforting to know that the chap's been cleared. I didn't want you spending time down there with him if he—"

"What do you mean he's been cleared?"

Her father blinked. "Why, the FBI made an arrest today, didn't they? I just read in the paper that—"

"What paper?" Abby demanded, shoving out of her chair and ignoring Luke Lazurnovich's dawning grin. "Where is it?"

"In the study," Father called after her. "It's—"

Abby slammed out of the dining room and ran across the hall into her father's oak-paneled study. The local newspaper had been abandoned on a leather ottoman, and Abby frantically scrabbled through the sheets until she found the front page. She could hardly hold it still enough to read the headlines.

WEST VIRGINIA DISTILLERY OWNER CHARGED WITH TAINTING PEANUT BUTTER.

Gasping, half-sobbing, Abby scanned down through the article. *Michael Piper, cousin of Robert Piper and the president of Piper's Peanut Butter, accompanied the accused to the arraignment today. Story con't. on page 6.*

Abby tore through the pages, and suddenly there was Mick's face, not seeming the least bit like himself. Yes, he did look like a tormented Heathcliff, his eyes dark and devoid of his usual cheer, his mouth straight and tense. He was standing just behind his cousin Rob, who looked as though he was in shock—ill and half-angry. There were huge circles under Rob's pouchy eyes, and his usually dapper suit looked rumpled. He had half-turned to Mick, as if asking for support. Or perhaps forgiveness.

Abby did not hear her father come into the room and close the door. "Abigail?"

"I'm sorry," she said, though her voice was strained. "I didn't mean to make a scene."

"Your mother likes a little drama at her table now and then." He perched on the edge of the desk and looked pensively down at his daughter. "Are you going to let me help this time?"

Abby stayed on the ottoman below him. Her eyes were full of tears, she knew, but she tried to smile and shook her head. "I don't know what you mean, Father."

With false gruffness, he said, "Come on. Out with it."

Abby put her hand to her brow and tried to massage the tension away. Her voice was wavery. "Can I ask you something, Daddy? Something important?"

"How could I refuse? You haven't called me that name in years."

She laughed nervously and darted a look upward. "You said before you sent me to see the Pipers that I should go to see what the—the country folk could teach me. What did you mean, Daddy? Have I turned into a heartless person or something?"

He reached down and took her hand. "Of course not, Abby. But you had learned to hide your heart, I think, and keep it locked up tightly. From what I had heard about the Piper family, they wear their hearts on their sleeves—right out in the open, without pretending."

Squeezing his larger hand for all she was worth, she asked, "Do I pretend too much?"

"We all pretend. But that episode you were involved in when you were working for the newspaper—that bothered you a lot, I knew, even though you pretended to have steady nerves like your reporter friend. I realized that I didn't want you to turn out the way your mother and I have—stuffy and wishing we had more."

"Oh, Daddy!" Abby flung herself into her father's arms. She felt like Dorothy returning from Oz and discovering that she had what she wanted all along. "Daddy, I love you so much!"

He hugged her back, laughing over her head. "I didn't bargain for this, my girl! What's happened? Have you fallen in love with one of them?"

"Yes, yes—the one who was innocent. I've fallen hard, and now I've hurt him very badly. I criticized the thing he holds most dear, and I—I feel terrible."

He eased her away. "Sorry for yourself, you mean?"

"Yes, I suppose. But mostly sorry for what I did to him." Abby bit her lip. "I was awfully mean."

"You'll have to apologize."

"I know. But not yet. I'm *afraid*."

"Would you like some fatherly advice? Get it over with, my dearest daughter." He reached for the oblong mahogany box that contained his private telephone. He pushed it toward the edge of the desk and Abby's hand. "Call him now."

Abby looked uncertainly at the phone and then hugged her father once more. "All right, I'll try. I've got to work up my courage first, though. You're a darling."

"I'm a hungry darling," he said, going gruff again. His actions belied his curmudgeon tone, however, as he used his perfect handkerchief to wipe Abby's streaked mascara from under her eyes. Then, lightly, he said, "If you're going to start calling long distance, I'll get back to our dinner guests."

But as her father went out into the hallway, he nearly collided with Joanna, who had been scuttling along the hallway at top speed.

"Oh, Mr. Vanderbine, sir," said the breathless maid, "there's a gentleman at the door, sir, who would like to speak with you if it's convenient, sir. He says he's looking for Miss Abigail, sir."

Abby went quickly to the doorway. *"Me?"*

"Joanna, did you tell him that Abigail was here?"

"No, sir, I—"

Abby bolted away from them, hurrying down the marble floor with her heart fairly pounding in her ears. It had to be. It had to be! Please, please, let it be Mick!

It was. He was standing in the foyer, his hands thrust into his trouser pockets, his head tilted away from her as he studied a painting on the wall. He heard her footsteps and turned.

Abby wanted to fling herself into his arms, laughing with joy and crying his name over and over. But his face—that terrible tautness again—stopped her. Abby faltered to a stop, barely three yards away. She knew that her eyes must have been huge and probably showing evidence of her tears. It took every iota of poise to collect herself.

"Mick." That was all she could say.

"Hello, Abby."

The tone of his voice told her nothing. He looked tall and lean in the hallway, tougher than most of the men that had passed through the Vanderbine doors. It was strange to see him standing in the opulently decorated foyer of her parents' home the way all her high-school prom dates had stood. But Mick didn't exactly look ill at ease or out of place there. It registered in Abby's mind that Mick would look rock steady in any setting. He was his own man, and at the moment he looked quite untouchable. He had not come with his hat in his hand to wheedle her back into his life. He had come with a purpose, Abby could see. But she couldn't imagine what it was.

He looked handsome as ever. He had deigned to exchange his jeans and usual flannel shirt for a pair of khaki trousers and a tweed sports coat, but he looked just as tough as he did dressed for a mean round of one-on-one. His dark hair was ruffled, as if he had deliberately not combed it before gaining entrance to the house. His face looked tired, so different from the first time Abby met him. He looked older now, as if the past few days had acted like a decade on his soul. He controlled himself absolutely, however. There was no sign of weakness.

Abby hugged herself. The door was closed, but she felt as if the evening air from outside was chilling her to the bone. "I didn't expect you to—to be here."

"No, I suppose not." Shortly, he explained, "I tried to call, but you weren't answering at the number that's listed. I thought—well, I took a chance on finding you at this address."

He paused then and glanced pointedly up at the curved ceiling, an intricate mosaic made of tiny glazed tiles that had been imported from Portugal. A huge Waterford chandelier sparkled over his head, too, and his gaze took in that as well as a gigantic portrait of Abby's great-grandfather Vanderbine—complete with watch chain and faithful dog—that hung on the wall opposite the double doors. He summed up the grandeur of the entry hall succinctly by saying simply, "Not bad."

"I don't live here," Abby said hastily. "This house belongs to my parents."

"But you were raised here?" he asked, deliberately emphasizing the twang of his home state.

"Well—" She hesitated, having heard the tone of his voice. A flicker of anger ignited inside her. If Mick had come to rub her nose in her sophistication again, she wouldn't stand for it. She couldn't help what kind of family she had been born into. Mick was deliberately drawing the lines of separation between them. Stiffening her back, Abby said, "Yes, as a matter of fact, I *was* brought up here. Would you like a tour of the house?"

"No," he said, piercing her gaze with his. "I'll pass, thank you."

Though she was angry inside, Abby felt sorry that she had been sarcastic. Perhaps Mick was paying her back for making cutting remarks about *his* family. She deserved worse punishment from him, she knew. She stood frozen for a moment, holding his gaze and wondering how she was supposed to carry off this kind of scene without embarrassing herself. Already there was a huge lump in her throat. She couldn't speak.

Mick took in her appearance finally, lingering on the apple-green dress and the way it clung to her narrow waist. He said, "You certainly look like the lady of the mansion, Miss Vanderbine."

Swiftly, Abby began, "If you've come to get an apology out of me, Mick, I can say right now that—"

"No, I didn't come for that," he said, voice sharp. "I have some things to say to you instead."

"Would you like to come in and sit down?"

"No," he said quickly, and he glanced around the

beautiful foyer again. "This isn't my style, and you're having a party. I'll just say my piece and go."

He was uncomfortable, Abby realized. He was damned if he would show it, but he didn't feel right. With a momentary surge of sympathy, she said, "Well, we can take a walk, if you like. I'll get my coat."

"Don't bother. I won't take up that much of your time."

Abby glared at him. So much for sympathy! He must be really furious with her if he could manage to sound so cold. For fear she was going to break down and act like a weak female idiot in front of him, Abby brushed past Mick and said, "Let's talk outside, at least. This place echoes, and I'd rather that the help not overhear any of this."

"The help?" he asked, making it to the door in time to open it for her. Mocking, he said, "You mean the servants?"

Abby stepped out onto the flagstone loggia and swung on him almost immediately. "Yes, the servants. The butler and the maids and the footmen—all of them! Is this what you wanted, Mick? To come and be sarcastic about my family? Since you've got the all-American mother and father who stand by your side to the bitter end—"

"Stop it," he snapped, his voice rising once they were safely outside and alone in the half-darkness. "I don't want to fight that battle all over again. We hurt each other enough the last time."

Abby tried not to shiver. She hugged herself and faced him, but she couldn't look him in the eye. "All right," she said, voice subdued. "What did you come to say?"

Mick hesitated. "I—Rob was arrested and charged today."

"Yes, I just saw the newspaper."

"You were right about him," Mick said stiffly. "I couldn't listen to you when you told me about Rob. I didn't want to hear what you were saying, but I was wrong."

Good heavens, she thought. He had come to apologize to *her*.

When she did not respond, he continued, "I had to come to grips with a lot of things before I was—before I confronted Rob with what we knew. I talked with him last night, and today we went together to the FBI. Rob knew that what he had done was wrong, Abby. I want you to understand that he—he isn't a bad person."

"Just misguided?"

Mick almost snapped at her, but he apparently collected himself in time. He said steadily, "He had his priorities mixed up a little, I think. The competition between the two of us has been—well, it's been going on for a long time. Compounded with the fact that Rob was probably in love with Laura long before I married her . . ."

"That was just a theory," Abby said quickly. "I don't think you should take what I said about your wife too seriously."

"But you were right," Mike argued. "I knew even when I married her how much Rob had—cared for her. I felt guilty about stealing his girl even then. But—I don't know, maybe he held me responsible for her death somehow. He wanted to punish me, and he wanted to get his hands on a more profitable business. This scheme he cooked up could have satisfied both motives."

"Has he admitted those things?"

"Yes."

Abby could imagine the scene that the two cousins

must have gone through before all the facts came to light. It must have been terrible for Mick. No wonder he looked so drained. She wanted to console him, but it was clear that he was accepting nothing from her at this point. Keeping herself a safe six feet from him, she asked, "How did he do it?"

"How did he poison the peanut butter? There was a young kid at the university who did an internship at the distillery. About a year ago, Rob decided to go ahead with—with his scheme. He asked the kid to steal some penicillin from the lab supplies and then waited for the uproar over the theft to die down. About a month ago, Rob used his key, the one I had given him, to get into the plant late at night. The crew was taking their meal break at the time, he said. He chose several dozen jars at random and slipped the drug inside before they were filled with peanut butter."

"Then he waited for the jars to find their way to store shelves and for people with allergies to penicillin to start eating the stuff," Abby said.

"Right," Mick agreed. He added, "Rob explained everything to the police."

"Did you—" Abby stopped herself. She wasn't sure she wanted to know how the confession had come about. That had undoubtedly been just as painful for Mick as it had been for Rob—perhaps even more so.

"I asked Rob to go to the authorities," Mick said, guessing her thoughts. "He refused at first, and there was a lot of crazy talk about running away from—from what he had done. We stayed up most of the night deciding what to do."

"We?" Abby asked. "You and Rob or the whole Piper clan?"

"All of us," Mick agreed, sounding dangerous once again. "We're a very close family, Abby. We accept each other, warts and all. None of us is going to reject Rob just because he's made a mistake."

"His 'mistake,' as you call it," Abby said bitterly, "nearly cost you your business and your freedom."

Mick shrugged. "I forgive him."

"Because he's part of your family?"

"Yes," said Mick. "I love him."

Abby sighed. Yes, she had known all along that Mick wouldn't be able to work up any anger against his cousin, no matter how heinous the crimes were. The bond between the members of the Piper family was very, very strong. Now Abby understood that bond, and she wished that her own family was just as tightly held together. She envied the Pipers.

"So," Mick continued with the story, "when we had gone to the police and given all the information, I knew I had one more loose string to tie up before everything was over."

"What was that?"

"To come apologize to you," he said calmly. "I said some pretty uncomplimentary stuff before you left, and I'm sorry. I got you involved in the first place, too, and I shouldn't have. I should have made you go home after that first day, but I—well, I didn't. I'm sorry for that, too."

"I got myself involved," Abby said tightly. "You don't need to take the blame for that."

"Well, I should have seen a lot sooner that you were unwilling—I mean, that you were there for the wrong reasons. If I could—"

"What reason did you think I had?" Abby interrupted.

Mick looked at her and blinked. "I don't know exactly. But it should have been obvious to me that a classy lady like you had no business hanging around Blue Creek, West Virginia, unless it was for—I don't know."

"Unless it was for what?"

Mick shrugged. "Sex?"

Abby would have laughed if she could. The possibility that Abigail Vanderbine might be jet-setting around the nation looking for sexual partners was so amazingly impossible that it was funny. It made Abby sad that Mick could imagine her capable of such a motive. She shook her head. "Do you really believe that, Mick?"

"I don't know what to believe," he said flatly. "The family I thought was indestructible is now in an uproar, and you—I don't understand you at all, Abby. I thought I had you all figured out, and then you changed gears or something. I thought you were a class act, but with a gentle, vulnerable side that—well, I guess I should have seen you in this setting before. This is where you belong, isn't it? A palatial house and silk dresses and a housemaid to answer your door."

Abby shook her head, hugging herself to keep the shivering at bay. Any second she was going to cry, and that fact made her feel even angrier with herself. She longed to explain how she was infinitely more comfortable in jeans and his own dopey flannel shirts. She would never manage to get all those words out, though. Instead, she said inadequately, "I'm not the woman you thought I was, Mick."

"That's obvious. I thought you were cool, all right, and talented and capable and maybe even—"

"A jet-set bitch?"

"I'm sorry I called you a bitch. I didn't mean that,

but I was—well, I won't make excuses." Mick took a breath and looked at her. "I didn't realize that you could be in—such control all the time, I guess. I went off the deep end, and all the time you were—well, more sophisticated than I was."

"Mick, I was not being absolutely honest with you," Abby began. "I tried to be the kind of woman that I thought you wanted."

"So you pretended." Mick considered that information, watching Abby struggle to say more. His face was cold and forbidding suddenly, and before she could continue, he asked abruptly, "Was it worth it?"

Stronger, Abby said, "Yes."

"You got what you wanted, then?" he demanded. "A fling with a country boy?"

"Mick, I—"

"Look," he interrupted, clearly not wanting to hear another word. "I don't pretend to understand what goes on in the minds of women these days. I've been out of circulation too long. But if you were happy with what you got while you were with me, then I guess I can live with that. It makes me feel pretty—I don't know." He shook his head wearily and passed his hand through his hair. "I suppose it was nice while it lasted, Miss Vanderbine."

Abby was silent. She couldn't explain without acting like a fool, and she was afraid that Mick would lose his temper. She was going to cry any second, and she couldn't face him like that.

"I think," he said finally, "that I'd better go back home and think about what's happened. I'm too much of a hillbilly to be running around loose with worldly people like you. You'd better go inside and get warm again. I'll call—no, I think I'll just go home and stay there."

He was going to say good-bye. Any second he was going to say good-bye and walk away and down the sidewalk and disappear into the night. She was never going to see him again. He wasn't ever going to telephone her. He wanted to put a lot of distance between them as quickly as possible.

Abby wanted to hug him. She wanted to fly into his arms and hold him hard, keeping him with her forever. She almost did it. She nearly walked straight into his arms right then. But she stopped herself. Mick wouldn't stand for it, she was certain. He was too angry and disgusted and unhappy. He turned away and went down the steps.

Abby panicked. There had to be a way of keeping him there for a few minutes at least! She couldn't let him walk away without making him understand.

After him, she called, "Have you eaten?"

He paused and turned. "What?"

"Have you had dinner yet?" she asked, though her voice was probably no louder than a whisper. "I—I certainly owe you a meal after all the time I spent with you. I—I'll make you a peanut-butter sandwich."

Distinctly, he said, "You haven't got any peanut butter in this house, Miss Vanderbine. People like you don't like peanut butter."

Abby took a breath, but it came out like a sob. "I l-love peanut butter, Mick."

He must have seen the tears glisten on her cheek, because he stopped still and didn't move for the longest moment Abby had ever endured. Slowly, then, he came back into the light, as if not quite believing. "Abby . . ." he began, and his voice was different.

"I do," she said desperately. "I love it. It's sweet and good and nutritious and it sticks to your ribs and—it's a lot like you are, Mick. The all-American good guy, and I—I—"

"Abby!" he said, coming back up the steps. There was surprise written all over his face.

"And I love you, too, Mick," she said, stumbling forward and straight into his arms. "You're so sweet, and I'm sorry that I did anything that made you feel differently about Rob and your family. I wish that you wouldn't leave—I'll be heartsick if you go away like this. I—I'll make you a sandwich. Just stay, please. Stay and talk with me. I'm not sophisticated at all. I'm just a directionless, spoiled rich girl who—who feels she's got to put on an act, except when I was with you—I mean *truly* with you—I was myself then. Oh, Mick, you've got to believe me!"

He caught her up in his arms and hugged her so hard that her feet were off the ground. Her head was spinning and she thought she should be laughing, but there were tears instead, choking her so badly that she couldn't explain anymore.

"Darling Abby," said Mick, squeezing her as though he was afraid to let her go.

"I'm an idiot, and I can hardly talk when I—when I'm feeling like this. I'll try to explain, I promise, but Mick, please—"

"Don't cry," he said, and there was a twist in his voice. "I love you, too. The worst part about this whole mess was losing you when it was over. I couldn't let you go out of my life—not after the way we shouted and—and said those things to each other."

"I'm sorry I hurt you."

"You were right all along," he said. "I just didn't want to believe it, so I blamed you. And seeing you here in this house just made me think we were really wrong for each other, but—but I love you, Abby. I can't help it if we're different."

"We're not so different," she whispered breathlessly, holding him. "Maybe I pretended too long, but I—I'm not the snooty magazine dame you thought I was in the beginning. I'm just a woman who didn't know quite where she fit in—not until I met you, anyway. Mick, please—"

"I'm not going anywhere," he said against her hair. "Not without you."

He tilted her head then and kissed her cheeks dry, caressing her face, holding her tightly. He kissed her finally, and Abby wrapped her arms around his shoulders, warm and secure against his frame. Her trembling subsided, absorbed by Mick until their hearts were beating in swift synchronization.

They were still holding each other, murmuring in the half-light, when Abby's father pushed open the front door and came out into the night.

"So, Abigail," he said after a loud *harrumph*. "This is the man who's going to take you away from us?"

Abby didn't break out of Mick's embrace, but stood smiling tearily up at him. "No, Daddy, he's not exactly taking me anywhere. This is Mick. And something tells me that you two are going to get along just fine."

"Hello, sir."

"Call me Harry, son," replied Harcourt Ellsworth Vanderbine, looking jovial and very pleased with the scene before him. "Come inside, won't you? The silly maid ruined the dessert—she dropped the bombe, so to speak, so we're all going down to the kitchen to see what we can whip up for ourselves. How are you at making desserts?"

"Unless the recipe calls for peanut butter, Harry, I'm not much good, I'm afraid."

"I bought a jar today," announced Abby's father, much to his daughter's amazement. "It's pretty good stuff. I'd forgotten that. Come along. We'll see what we can make with it." He elbowed Mick affectionately and suggested, "Who knows? Maybe we'll come up with a way to make a peanut-butter-flavored wedding cake!"

Mick grinned and looked down at the woman in his arms. "Sounds delicious, doesn't it, dearest Abby?"

"Wonderful, darling. Absolutely wonderful."

Second Chance at Love ®

___	0-425-08015-3	PROMISE ME RAINBOWS #257 Joan Lancaster	$2.25
___	0-425-08016-1	RITES OF PASSION #258 Jacqueline Topaz	$2.25
___	0-425-08017-X	ONE IN A MILLION #259 Lee Williams	$2.25
___	0-425-08018-8	HEART OF GOLD #260 Liz Grady	$2.25
___	0-425-08019-6	AT LONG LAST LOVE #261 Carole Buck	$2.25
___	0-425-08150-8	EYE OF THE BEHOLDER #262 Kay Robbins	$2.25
___	0-425-08151-6	GENTLEMAN AT HEART #263 Elissa Curry	$2.25
___	0-425-08152-4	BY LOVE POSSESSED #264 Linda Barlow	$2.25
___	0-425-08153-2	WILDFIRE #265 Kelly Adams	$2.25
___	0-425-08154-0	PASSION'S DANCE #266 Lauren Fox	$2.25
___	0-425-08155-9	VENETIAN SUNRISE #267 Kate Nevins	$2.25
___	0-425-08199-0	THE STEELE TRAP #268 Betsy Osborne	$2.25
___	0-425-08200-8	LOVE PLAY #269 Carole Buck	$2.25
___	0-425-08201-6	CAN'T SAY NO #270 Jeanne Grant	$2.25
___	0-425-08202-4	A LITTLE NIGHT MUSIC #271 Lee Williams	$2.25
___	0-425-08203-2	A BIT OF DARING #272 Mary Haskell	$2.25
___	0-425-08204-0	THIEF OF HEARTS #273 Jan Mathews	$2.25
___	0-425-08284-9	MASTER TOUCH #274 Jasmine Craig	$2.25
___	0-425-08285-7	NIGHT OF A THOUSAND STARS #275 Petra Diamond	$2.25
___	0-425-08286-5	UNDERCOVER KISSES #276 Laine Allen	$2.25
___	0-425-08287-3	MAN TROUBLE #277 Elizabeth Henry	$2.25
___	0-425-08288-1	SUDDENLY THAT SUMMER #278 Jennifer Rose	$2.25
___	0-425-08289-X	SWEET ENCHANTMENT #279 Diana Mars	$2.25
___	0-425-08461-2	SUCH ROUGH SPLENDOR #280 Cinda Richards	$2.25
___	0-425-08462-0	WINDFLAME #281 Sarah Crewe	$2.25
___	0-425-08463-9	STORM AND STARLIGHT #282 Lauren Fox	$2.25
___	0-425-08464-7	HEART OF THE HUNTER #283 Liz Grady	$2.25
___	0-425-08465-5	LUCKY'S WOMAN #284 Delaney Devers	$2.25
___	0-425-08466-3	PORTRAIT OF A LADY #285 Elizabeth N. Kary	$2.25
___	0-425-08508-2	ANYTHING GOES #286 Diana Morgan	$2.25
___	0-425-08509-0	SOPHISTICATED LADY #287 Elissa Curry	$2.25
___	0-425-08510-4	THE PHOENIX HEART #288 Betsy Osborne	$2.25
___	0-425-08511-2	FALLEN ANGEL #289 Carole Buck	$2.25
___	0-425-08512-0	THE SWEETHEART TRUST #290 Hilary Cole	$2.25
___	0-425-08513-9	DEAR HEART #291 Lee Williams	$2.25

Prices may be slightly higher in Canada.

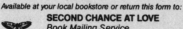

COMING NEXT MONTH
IN THE
SECOND CHANCE AT LOVE SERIES

SUNLIGHT AND SILVER #292 by Kelly Adams
Mississippi riverboat owner Noah Logan woos
pilot Jacy Jones with laughter and understanding, lulling
her with fond endearments and lazy days until
he threatens to commandeer her life!

PINK SATIN #293 by Jeanne Grant
Voluptuous Greer Lothrop feels safer offering
men chicken soup and sympathy than arousing their
impassioned longings. But neighbor Ryan McCullough
challenges her inhibitions and arouses shocking fantasies...

FORBIDDEN DREAM #294 by Karen Keast
Cade Sterling isn't merely Sarah Braden's former
brother-in-law—he's a captivating male!
Dare she defy social censure, her ex-husband's wrath, and
secret guilt to fulfill their forbidden longing?

LOVE WITH A PROPER STRANGER #295
by Christa Merlin
Anya Meredith is utterly infatuated with
stranger Brady Durant, but the mystery surrounding
a silver music box... and disturbing incidents...
suggest he's a conspirator in a sinister intrigue!

FORTUNE'S DARLING #296 by Frances Davies
Since winsome Andrew Wiswood, illustrious romance author,
can't write when not in love, literary agent
Joanna Simmons decides to seduce him herself, arousing him
to prodigious feats of penmanship...and passion!

LUCKY IN LOVE #297 by Jacqueline Topaz
Opposing strait-laced Alex Greene on legalized gambling,
devil-may-care Patti Lyon teases forth his more
adventurous spirit, while he tries to
seduce her into respectability!

QUESTIONNAIRE

1. How do you rate _____
   (please print TITLE)
   - ☐ excellent ☐ good
   - ☐ very good ☐ fair ☐ poor

2. How likely are you to purchase another book in this series?
   - ☐ definitely would purchase
   - ☐ probably would purchase
   - ☐ probably would not purchase
   - ☐ definitely would not purchase

3. How likely are you to purchase another book by this author?
   - ☐ definitely would purchase
   - ☐ probably would purchase
   - ☐ probably would not purchase
   - ☐ definitely would not purchase

4. How does this book compare to books in other contemporary romance lines?
   - ☐ much better
   - ☐ better
   - ☐ about the same
   - ☐ not as good
   - ☐ definitely not as good

5. Why did you buy this book? (Check as many as apply)
   - ☐ I have read other
     SECOND CHANCE AT LOVE romances
   - ☐ friend's recommendation
   - ☐ bookseller's recommendation
   - ☐ art on the front cover
   - ☐ description of the plot on the back cover
   - ☐ book review I read
   - ☐ other _____
     _____
     _____

(Continued...)

6. Please list your three favorite contemporary romance lines.

_____
_____

7. Please list your favorite authors of contemporary romance lines.

_____
_____
_____
_____
_____
_____

8. How many SECOND CHANCE AT LOVE romances have you read? _____

9. How many series romances like SECOND CHANCE AT LOVE do you <u>read</u> each month? _____

10. How many series romances like SECOND CHANCE AT LOVE do you <u>buy</u> each month? _____

11. Mind telling your age?
        ☐ under 18
        ☐ 18 to 30
        ☐ 31 to 45
        ☐ over 45

☐ Please check if you'd like to receive our <u>free</u> SECOND CHANCE AT LOVE Newsletter.

We hope you'll share your other ideas about romances with us on an additional sheet and attach it securely to this questionnaire.

• •

Fill in your name and address below:
Name _____
Street Address _____
City _____ State _____ Zip _____

Please return this questionnaire to:
  SECOND CHANCE AT LOVE
  The Berkley Publishing Group
  200 Madison Avenue, New York, New York 10016